TIGER MOTH

THE DUNG BEETLE
BANDITS

Librarian Reviewer
Allyson A. W. Lyga, MS
Library Media/Graphic Novel Consultant
Fulbright Memorial Fund Scholar, author

Reading Consultant
Elizabeth Stedem
Educator/Consultant, Colorado Springs, CO
MA in Elementary Education, University of Denver, CO

STONE ARCH BOOKS
MINNEAPOLIS   SAN DIEGO

Graphic Sparks are published by Stone Arch Books,
A Capstone Imprint
1710 Roe Crest Drive
North Mankato, Minnesota 56003
www.capstonepub.com

Library of Congress Cataloging-in-Publication Data
Reynolds, Aaron, 1970–
   The Dung Beetle Bandits / by Aaron Reynolds; illustrated by Erik Lervold.
   p. cm. — (Graphic Sparks. Tiger Moth)
   ISBN-13: 978-1-59889-317-5 (library binding)
   ISBN-10: 1-59889-317-3 (library binding)
   ISBN-13: 978-1-59889-412-7 (paperback)
   ISBN-10: 1-59889-412-9 (paperback)
   1. Graphic novels. I. Lervold, Erik. II. Title.
PN6727.R45D86 2007
741.5'973—dc22   2006028028

Summary: Tiger Moth and his sidekick, Kung Pow, visit a dung beetle ranch owned by
Tiger's Uncle Aphid. Thundering tarnation! The beetles are missing! It looks like the work
of that varmint rustler Stinky McCree. Tiger is convinced, however, that somewhere out
among the desert cacti, a darker evil lurks. And what's that gross stuff on Kung's hand?

Art Director: Heather Kindseth
Graphic Designer: Brann Garvey

Printed in the United States of America in North Mankato, Minnesota.
052018   000030

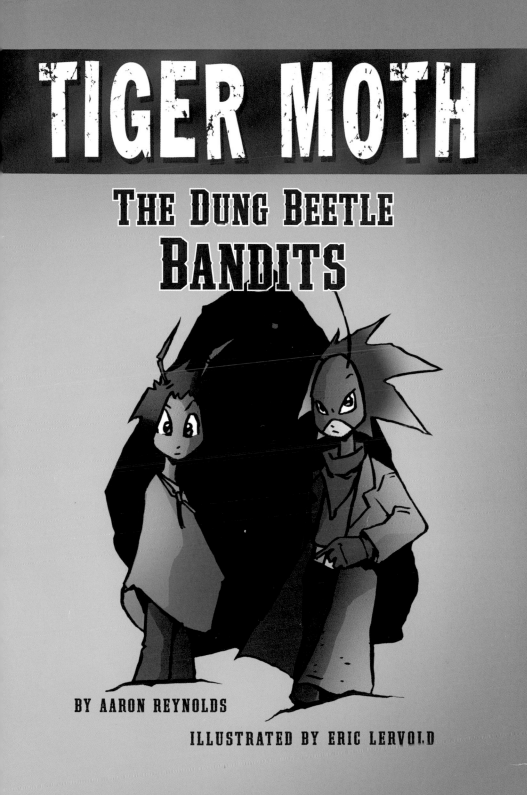

TIGER MOTH

THE DUNG BEETLE BANDITS

BY AARON REYNOLDS

ILLUSTRATED BY ERIC LERVOLD

Cast of Characters

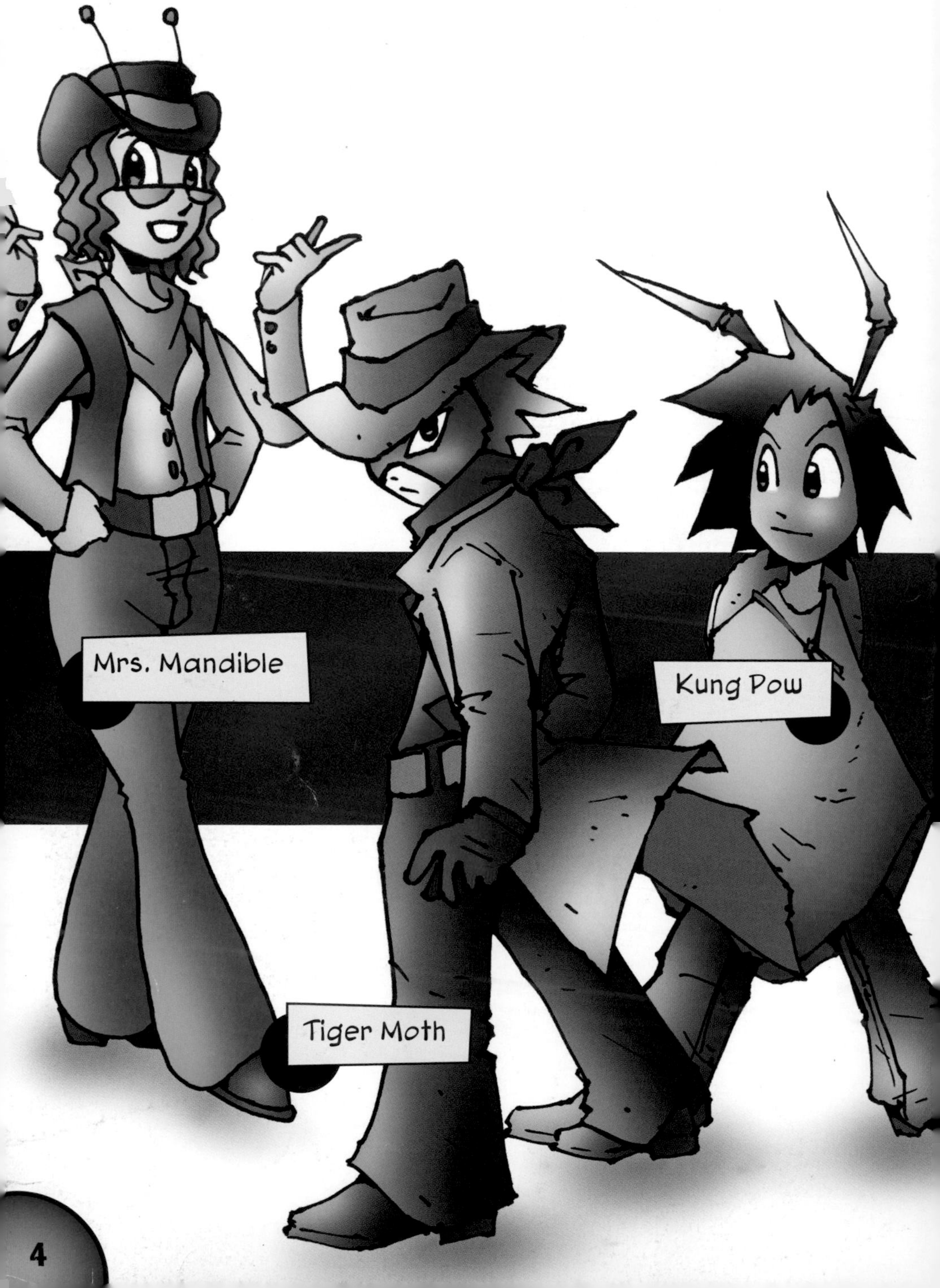
Mrs. Mandible
Kung Pow
Tiger Moth

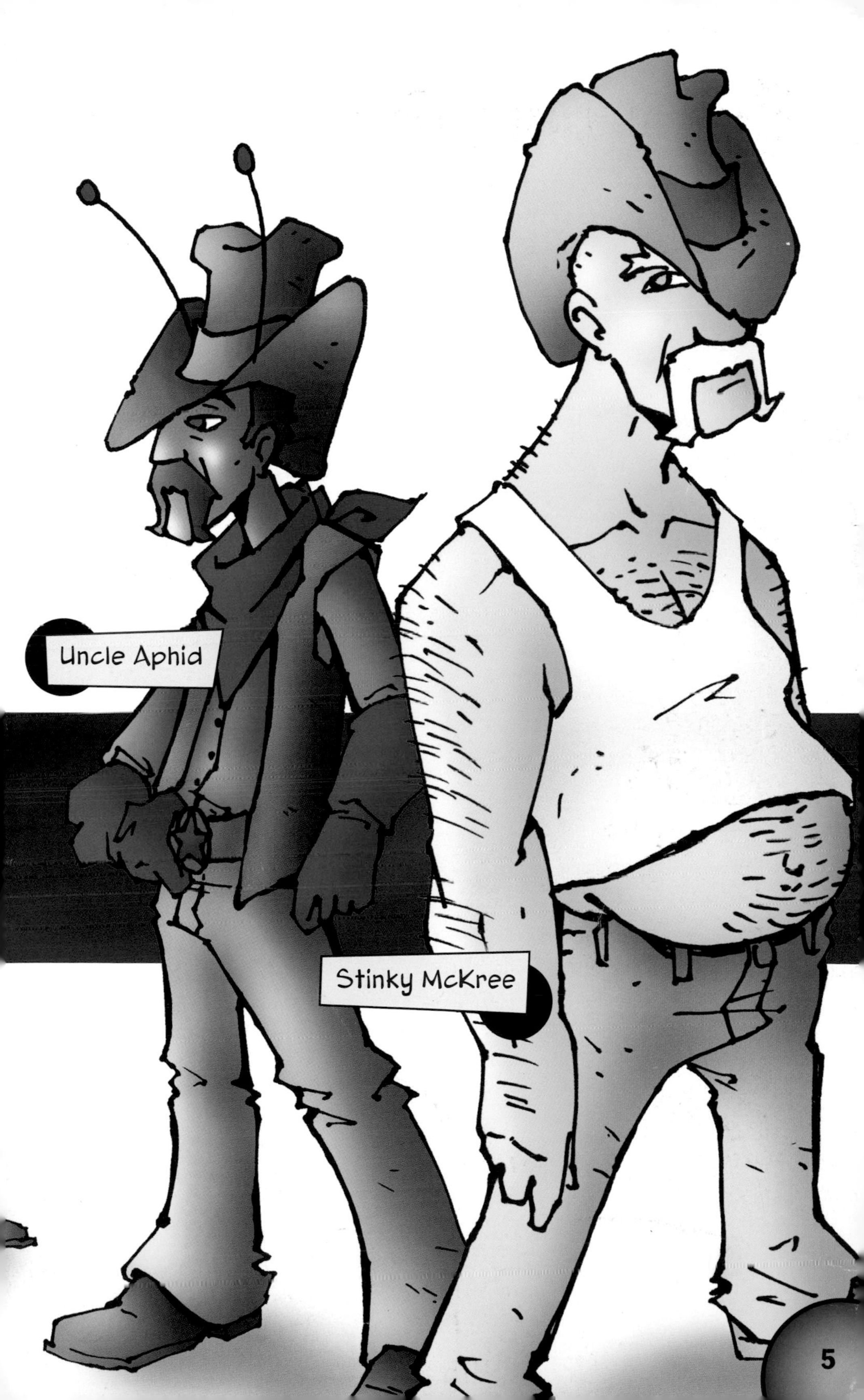
Uncle Aphid
Stinky McKree

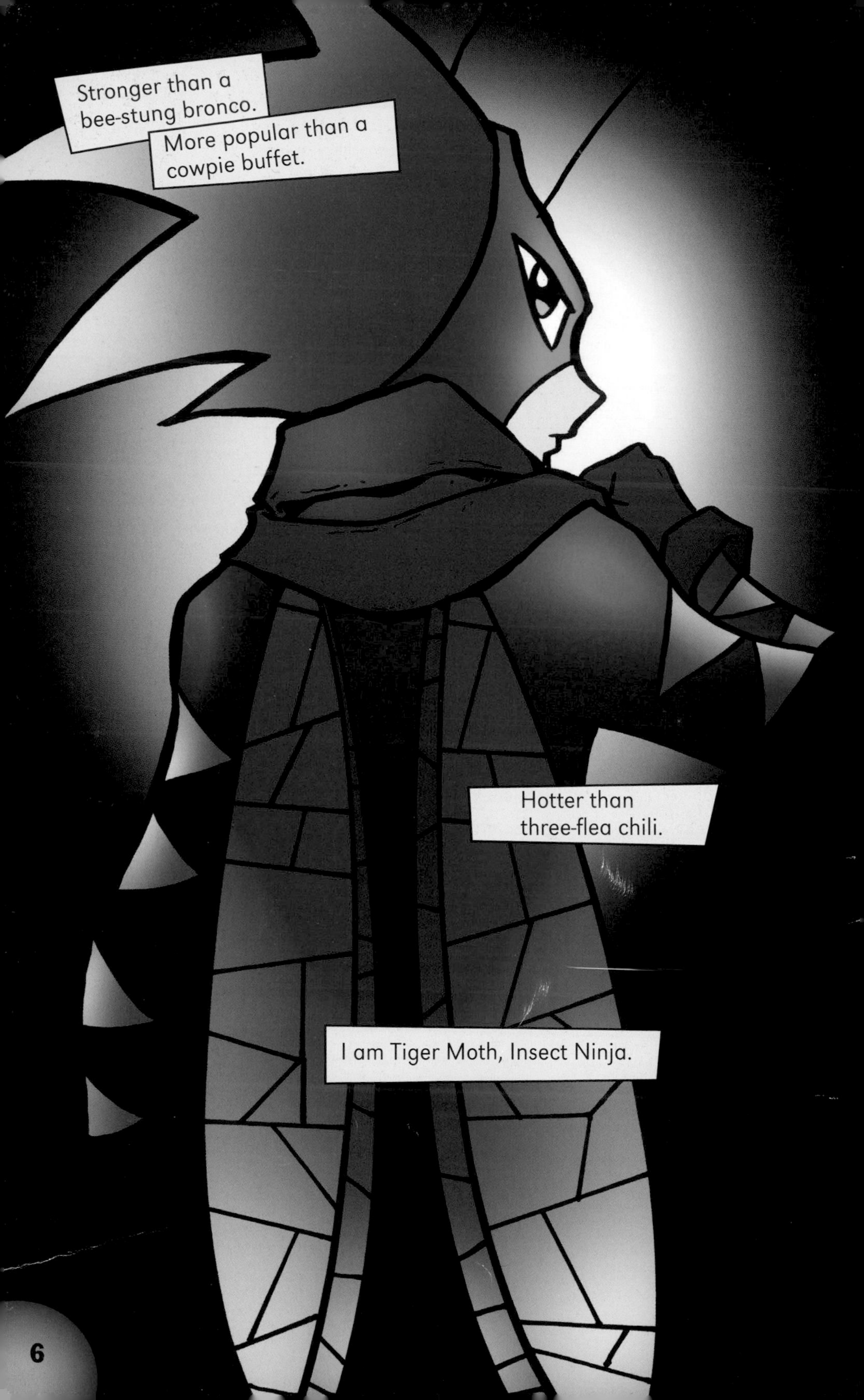
Stronger than a bee-stung bronco.
More popular than a cowpie buffet.
Hotter than three-flea chili.
I am Tiger Moth, Insect Ninja.

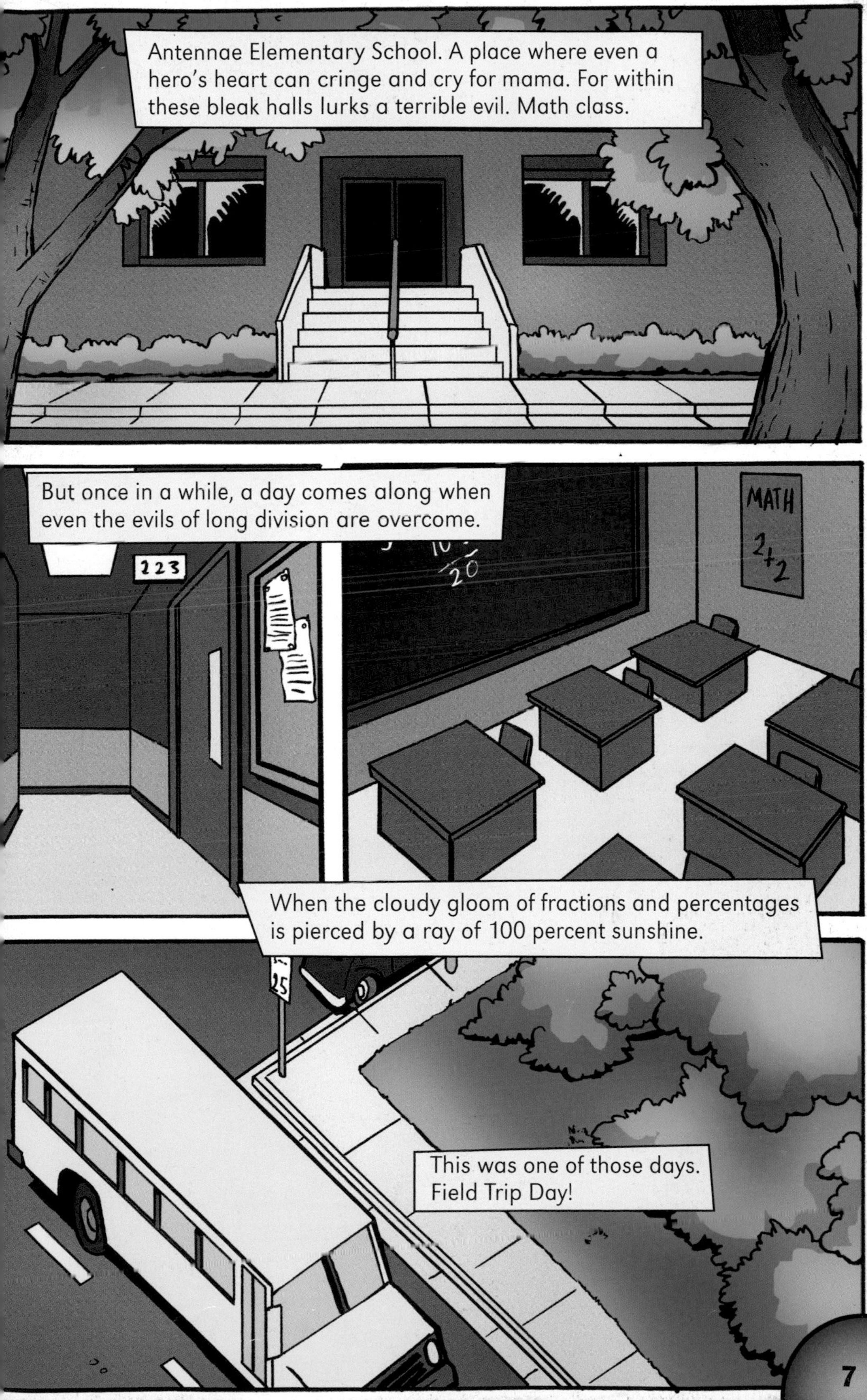
Antennae Elementary School. A place where even a hero's heart can cringe and cry for mama. For within these bleak halls lurks a terrible evil. Math class.
But once in a while, a day comes along when even the evils of long division are overcome.
223
MATH
When the cloudy gloom of fractions and percentages is pierced by a ray of 100 percent sunshine.
This was one of those days.
Field Trip Day!

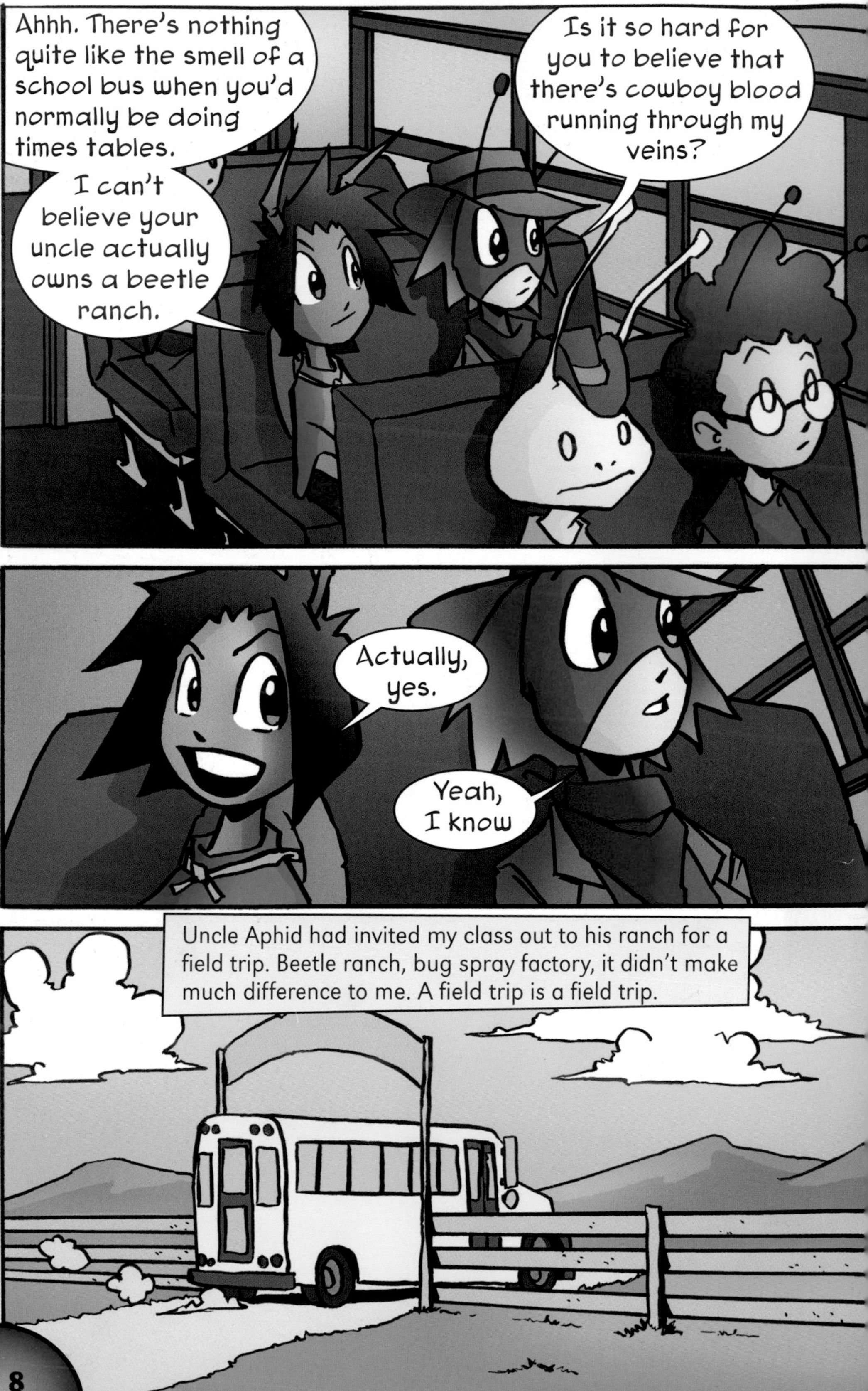
Ahhh. There's nothing quite like the smell of a school bus when you'd normally be doing times tables.
I can't believe your uncle actually owns a beetle ranch.
Is it so hard for you to believe that there's cowboy blood running through my veins?
Actually, yes.
Yeah, I know
Uncle Aphid had invited my class out to his ranch for a field trip. Beetle ranch, bug spray factory, it didn't make much difference to me. A field trip is a field trip.

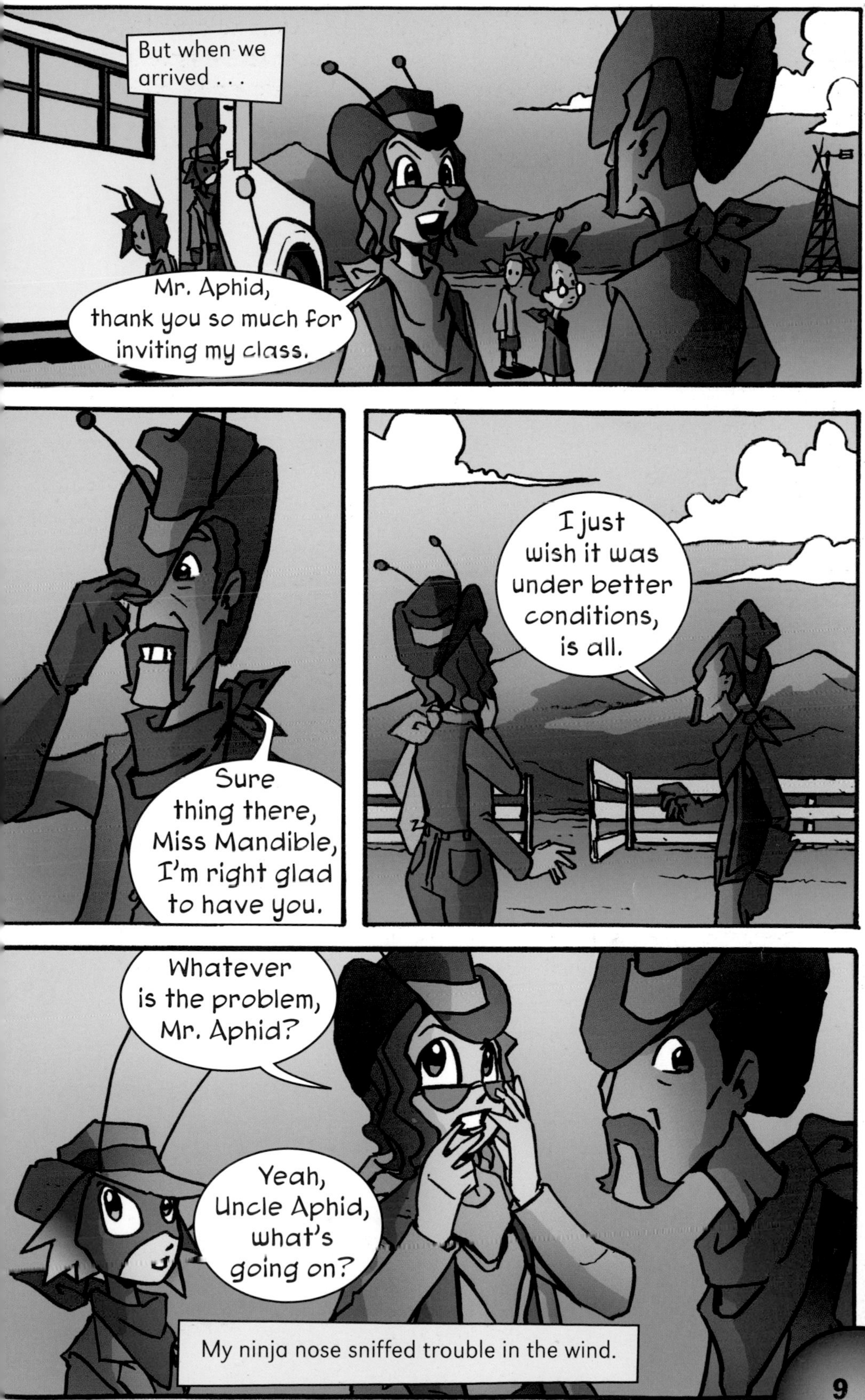

But when we arrived . . .
Mr. Aphid, thank you so much for inviting my class.
Sure thing there, Miss Mandible, I'm right glad to have you.
I just wish it was under better conditions, is all.
Whatever is the problem, Mr. Aphid?
Yeah, Uncle Aphid, what's going on?
My ninja nose sniffed trouble in the wind.

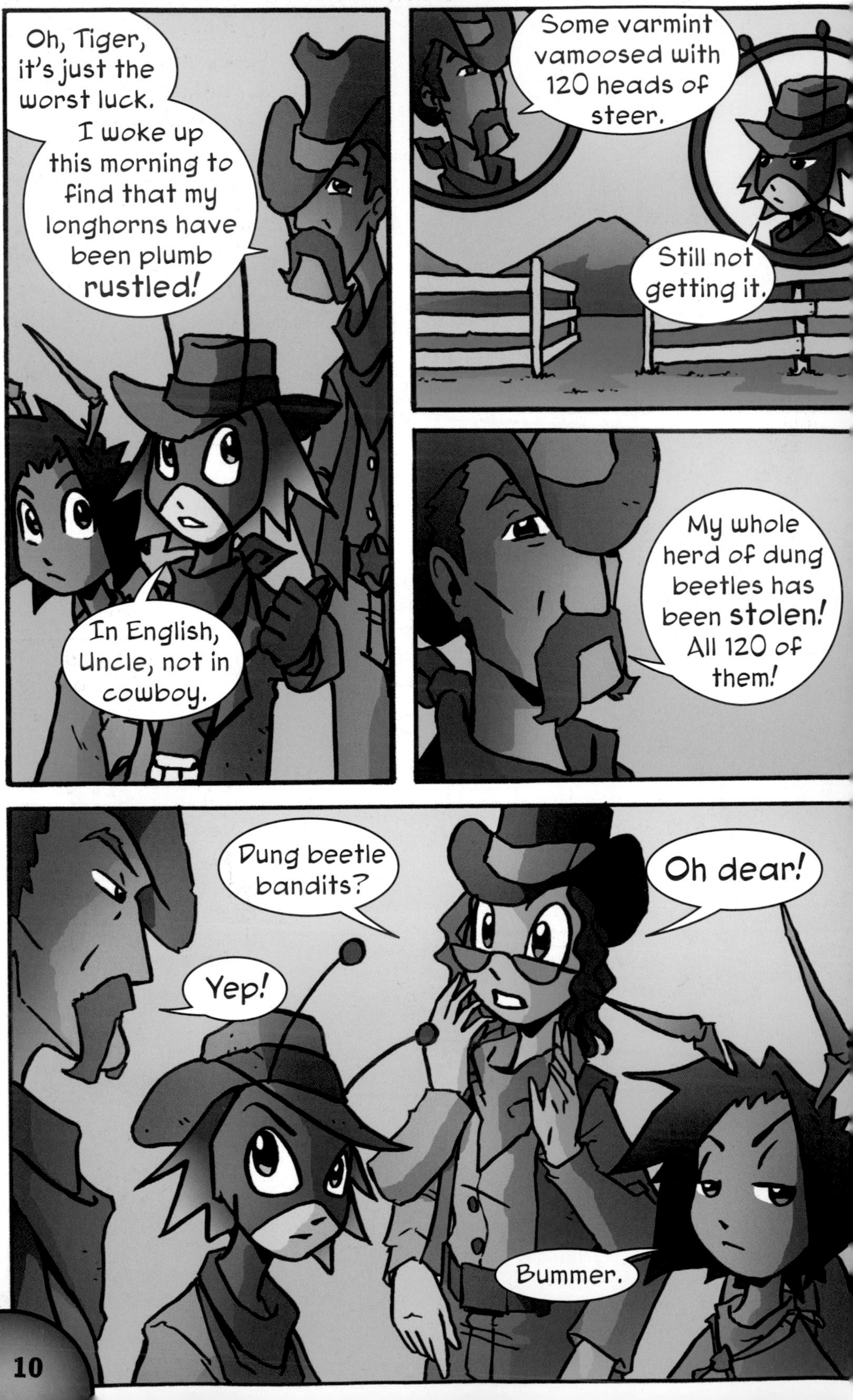
Oh, Tiger, it's just the worst luck.
I woke up this morning to find that my longhorns have been plumb rustled!
In English, Uncle, not in cowboy.
Some varmint vamoosed with 120 heads of steer.
Still not getting it.
My whole herd of dung beetles has been stolen! All 120 of them!
Dung beetle bandits?
Yep!
Oh dear!
Bummer.

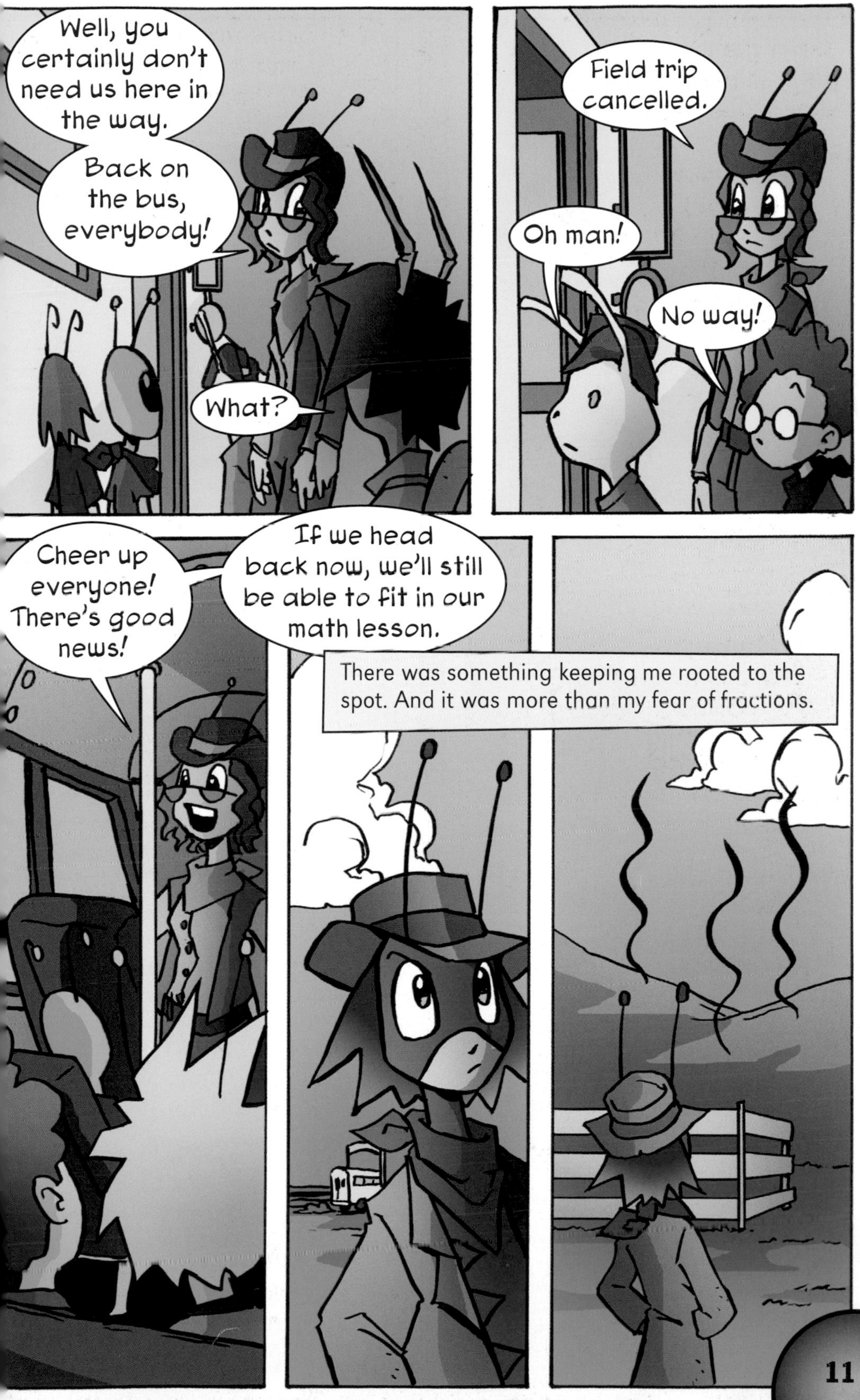
Well, you certainly don't need us here in the way.
Back on the bus, everybody!
What?
Field trip cancelled.
Oh man!
No way!
Cheer up everyone! There's good news!
If we head back now, we'll still be able to fit in our math lesson.
There was something keeping me rooted to the spot. And it was more than my fear of fractions.

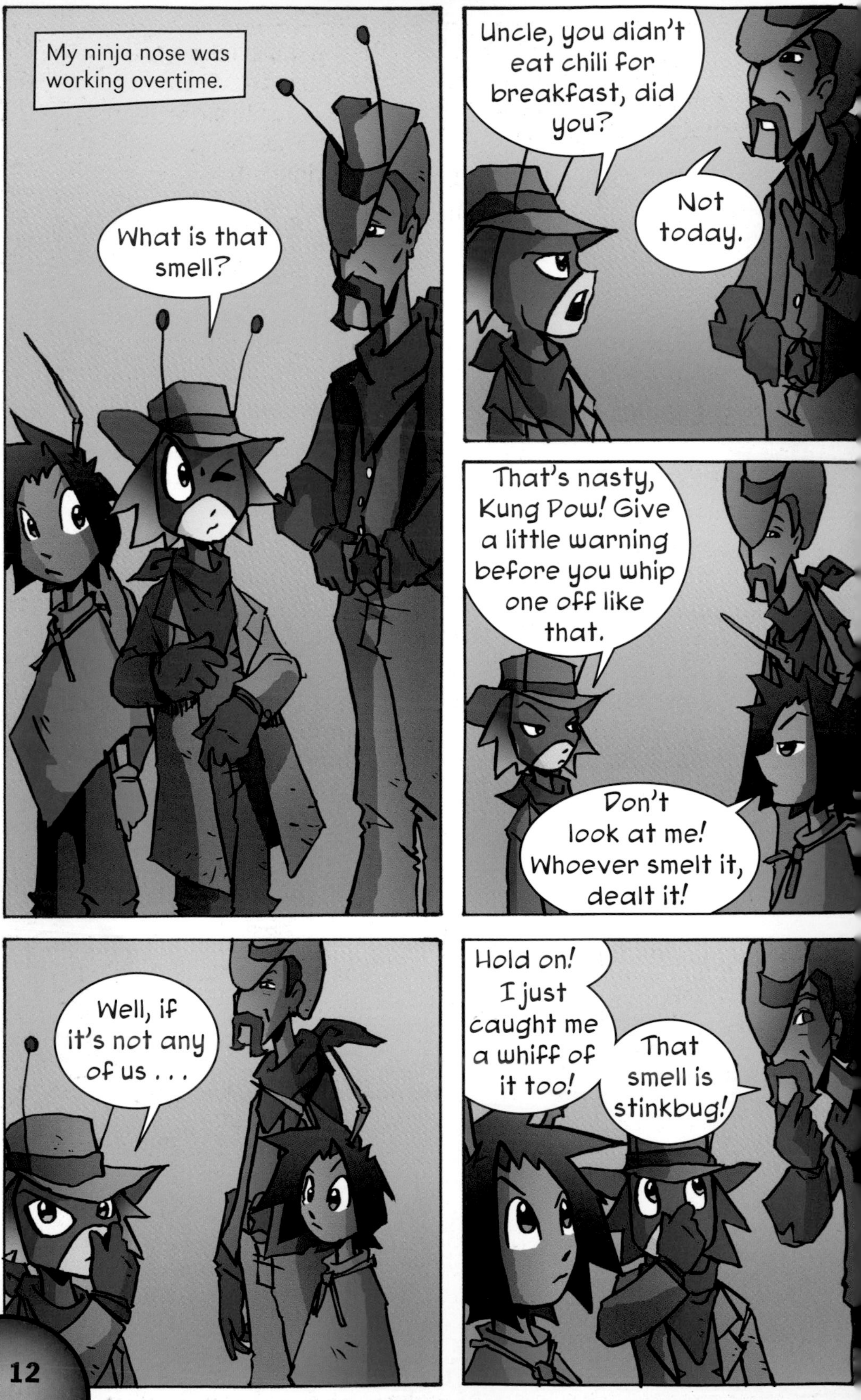
My ninja nose was working overtime.
What is that smell?
Uncle, you didn't eat chili for breakfast, did you?
Not today.
That's nasty, Kung Pow! Give a little warning before you whip one off like that.
Don't look at me! Whoever smelt it, dealt it!
Well, if it's not any of us . . .
Hold on! I just caught me a whiff of it too!
That smell is stinkbug!

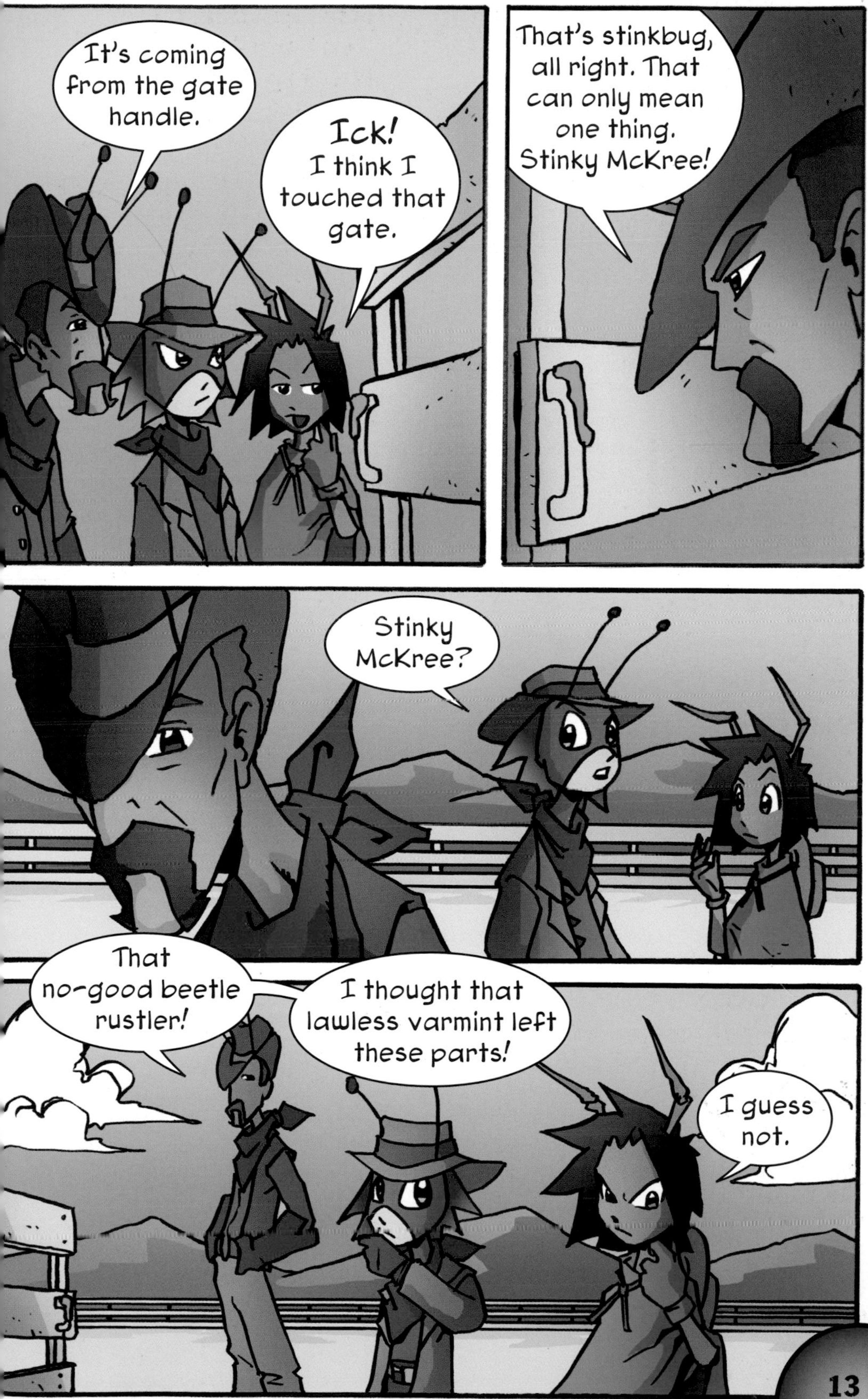
It's coming from the gate handle.
Ick! I think I touched that gate.
That's stinkbug, all right. That can only mean one thing. Stinky McKree!
Stinky McKree?
That no-good beetle rustler!
I thought that lawless varmint left these parts!
I guess not.

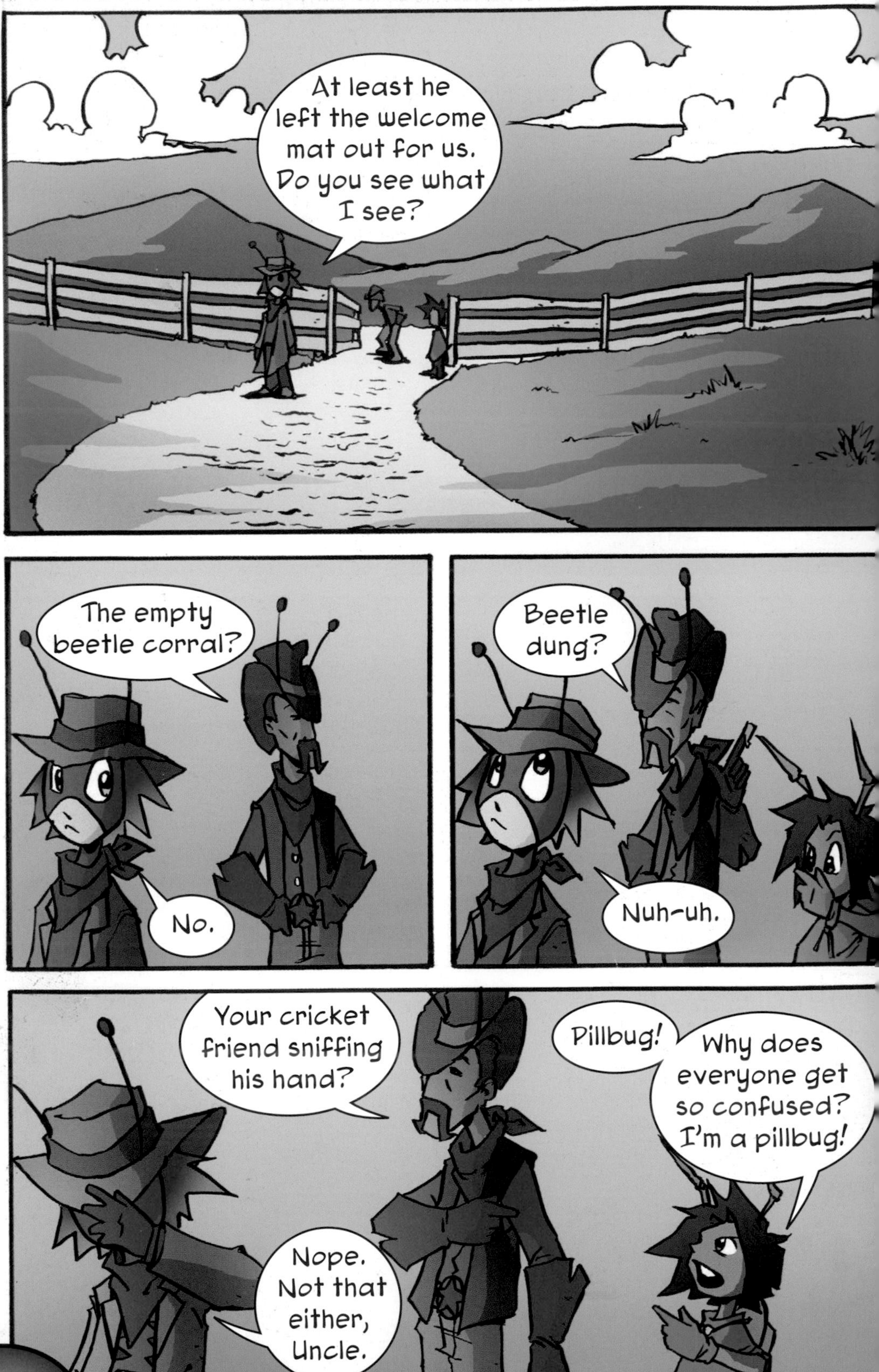
At least he left the welcome mat out for us. Do you see what I see?
The empty beetle corral?
No.
Beetle dung?
Nuh-uh.
Your cricket friend sniffing his hand?
Nope. Not that either, Uncle.
Pillbug!
Why does everyone get so confused? I'm a pillbug!

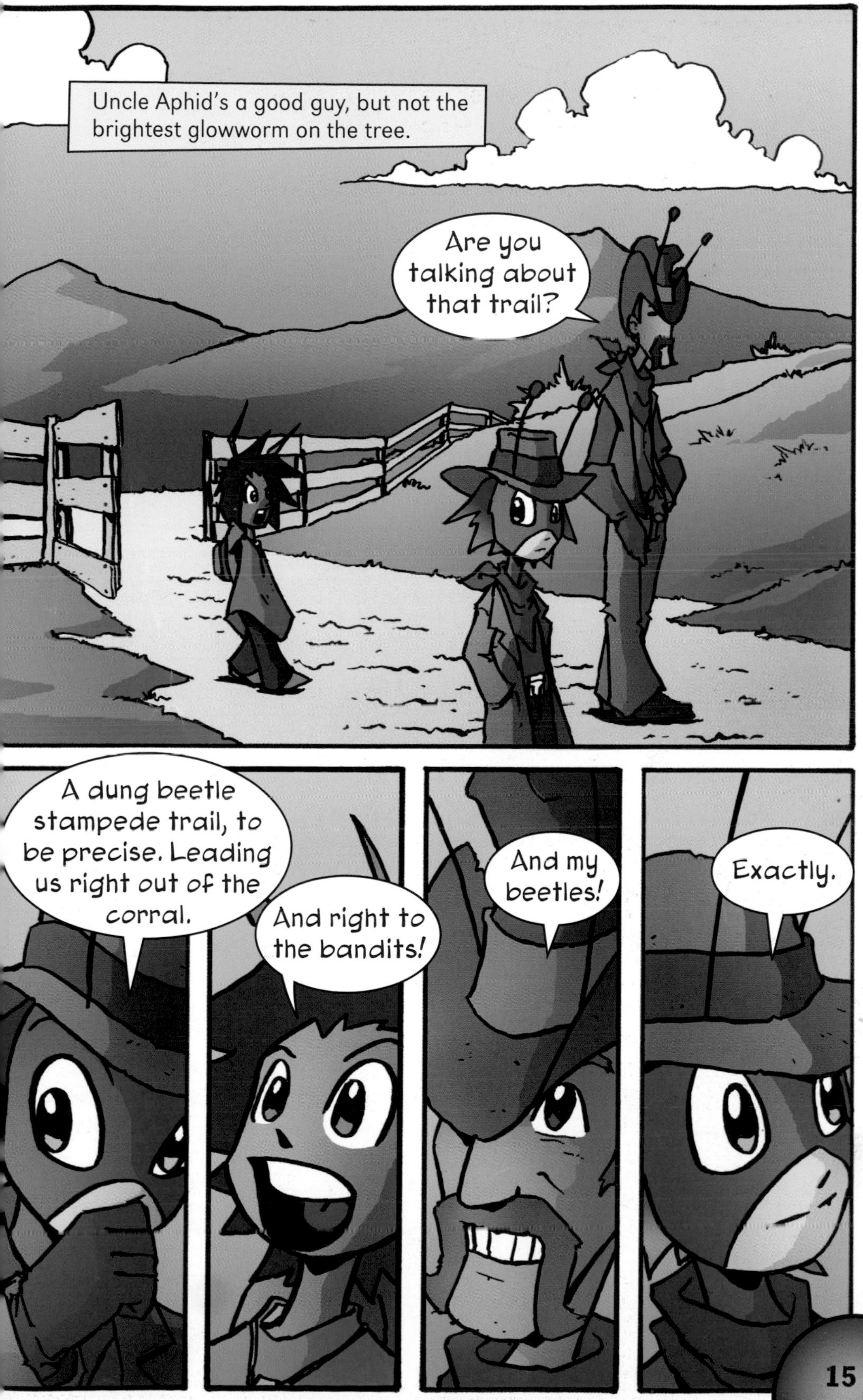
Uncle Aphid's a good guy, but not the brightest glowworm on the tree.
Are you talking about that trail?
A dung beetle stampede trail, to be precise. Leading us right out of the corral.
And right to the bandits!
And my beetles!
Exactly.

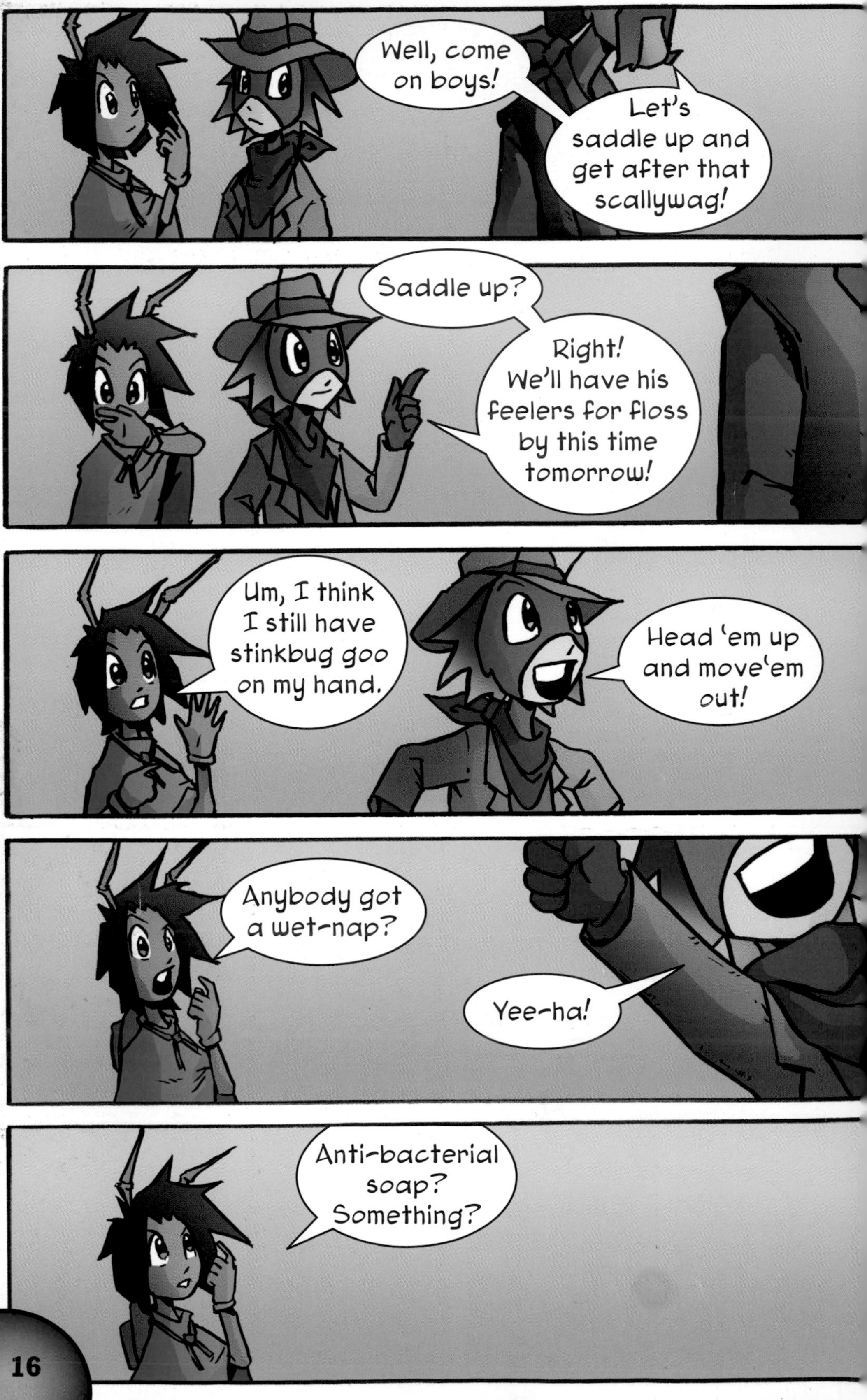
Well, come on boys!
Let's saddle up and get after that scallywag!
Saddle up?
Right! We'll have his feelers for floss by this time tomorrow!
Um, I think I still have stinkbug goo on my hand.
Head 'em up and move'em out!
Anybody got a wet-nap?
Yee-ha!
Anti-bacterial soap? Something?

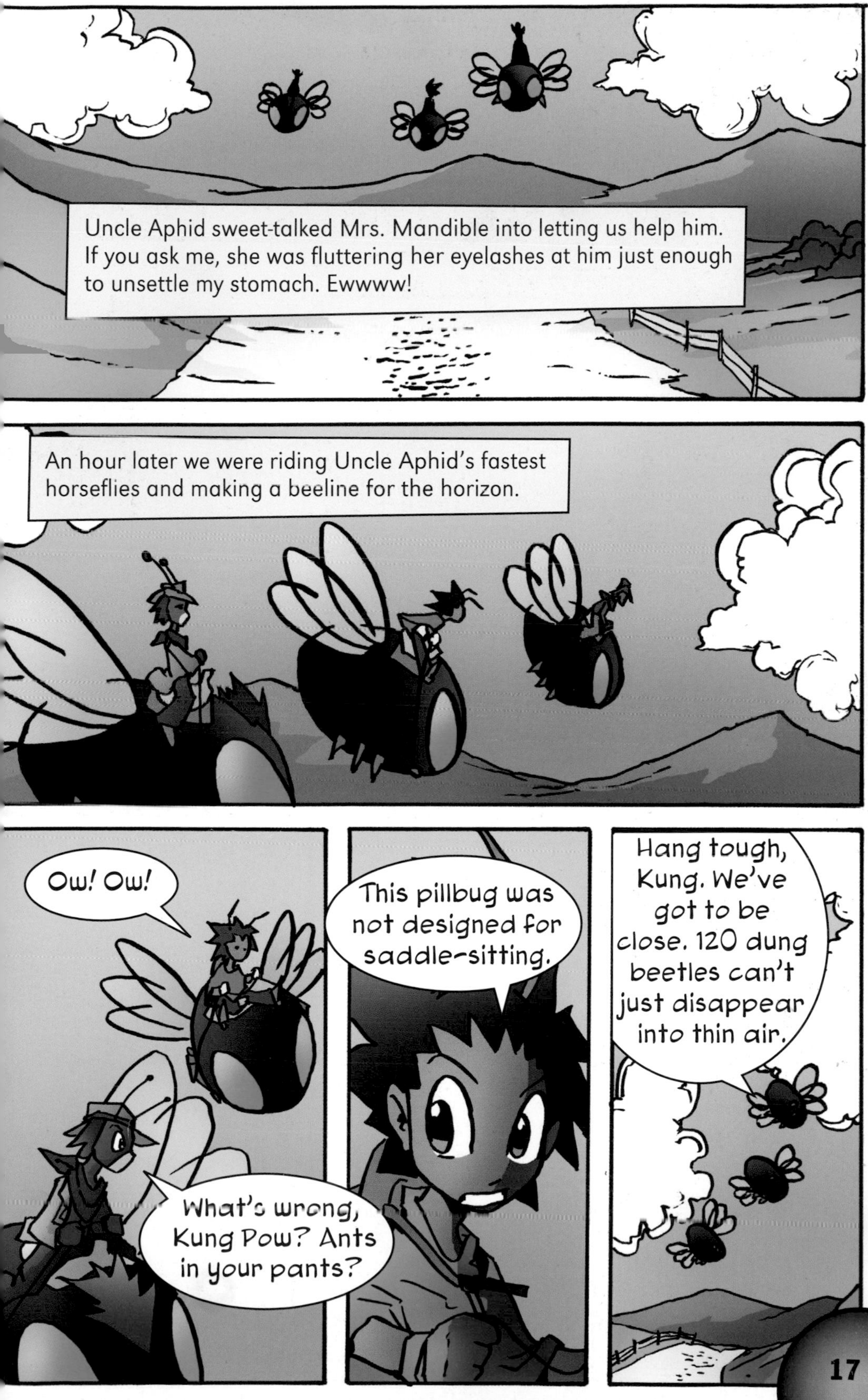
Uncle Aphid sweet-talked Mrs. Mandible into letting us help him. If you ask me, she was fluttering her eyelashes at him just enough to unsettle my stomach. Ewwww!
An hour later we were riding Uncle Aphid's fastest horseflies and making a beeline for the horizon.
Ow! Ow!
What's wrong, Kung Pow? Ants in your pants?
This pillbug was not designed for saddle-sitting.
Hang tough, Kung. We've got to be close. 120 dung beetles can't just disappear into thin air.

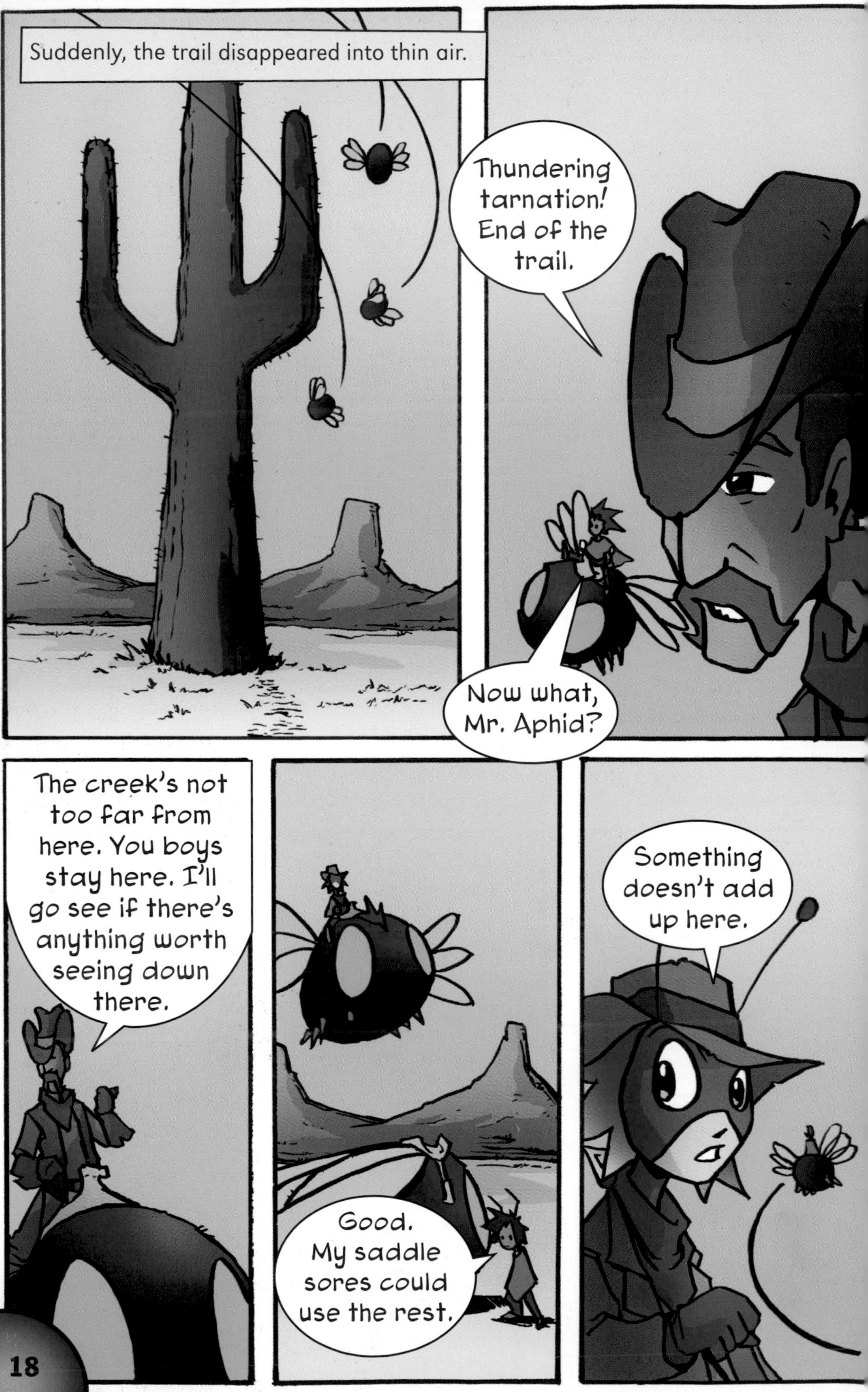
Suddenly, the trail disappeared into thin air.
Thundering tarnation! End of the trail.
Now what, Mr. Aphid?
The creek's not too far from here. You boys stay here. I'll go see if there's anything worth seeing down there.
Good. My saddle sores could use the rest.
Something doesn't add up here.

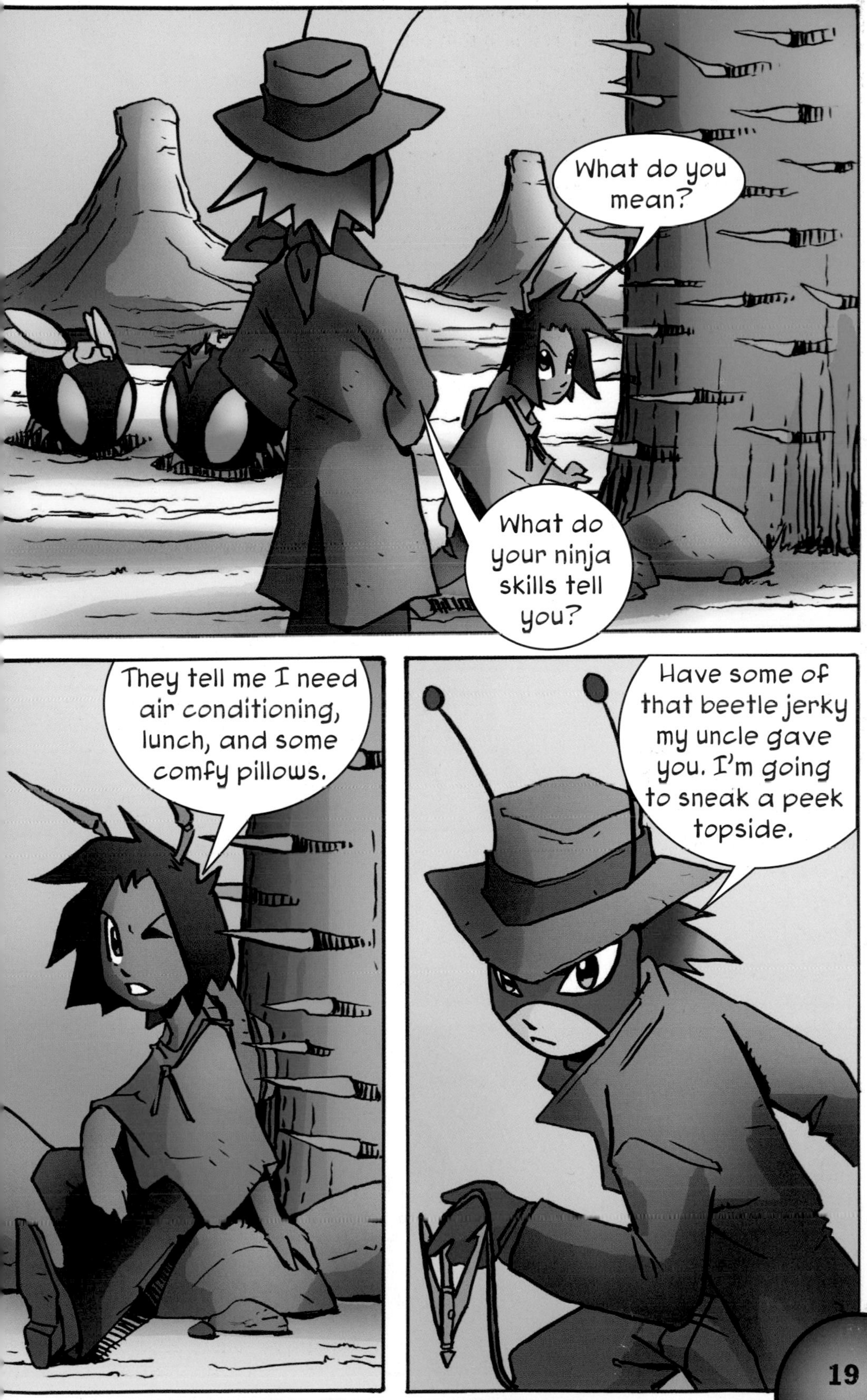
What do you mean?
What do your ninja skills tell you?
They tell me I need air conditioning, lunch, and some comfy pillows.
Have some of that beetle jerky my uncle gave you. I'm going to sneak a peek topside.

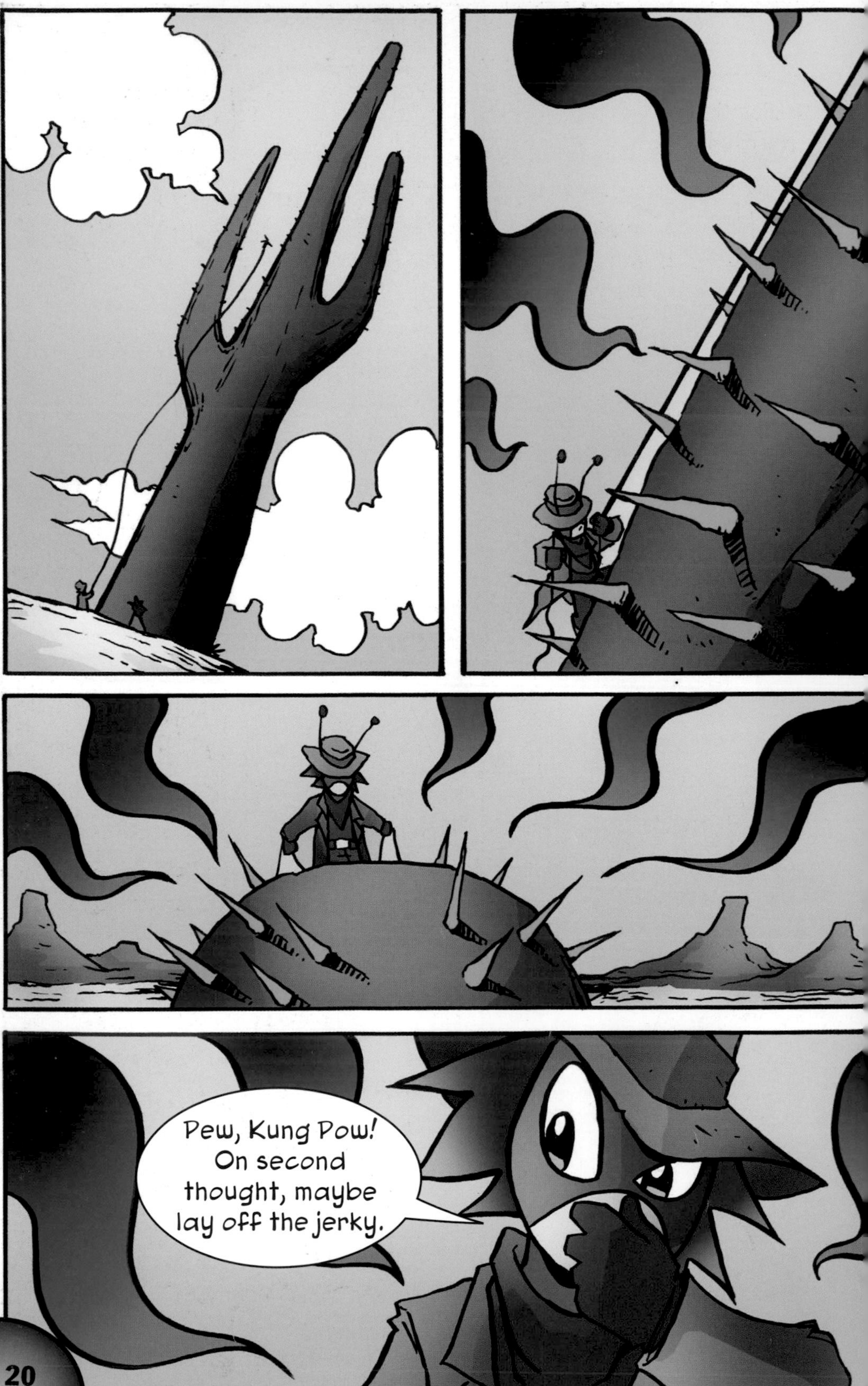
Pew, Kung Pow! On second thought, maybe lay off the jerky.

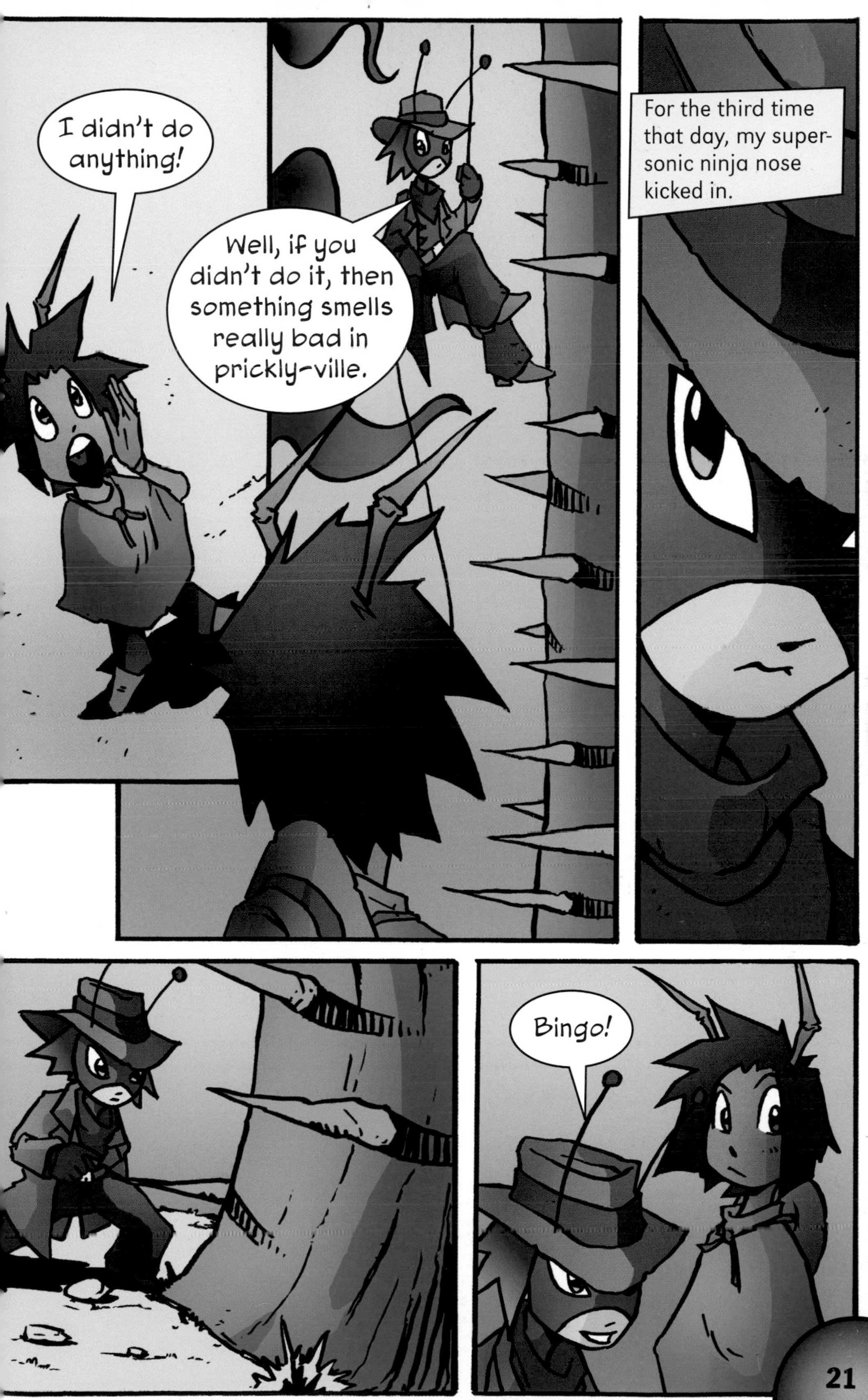
I didn't do anything!
Well, if you didn't do it, then something smells really bad in prickly-ville.
For the third time that day, my super-sonic ninja nose kicked in.
Bingo!

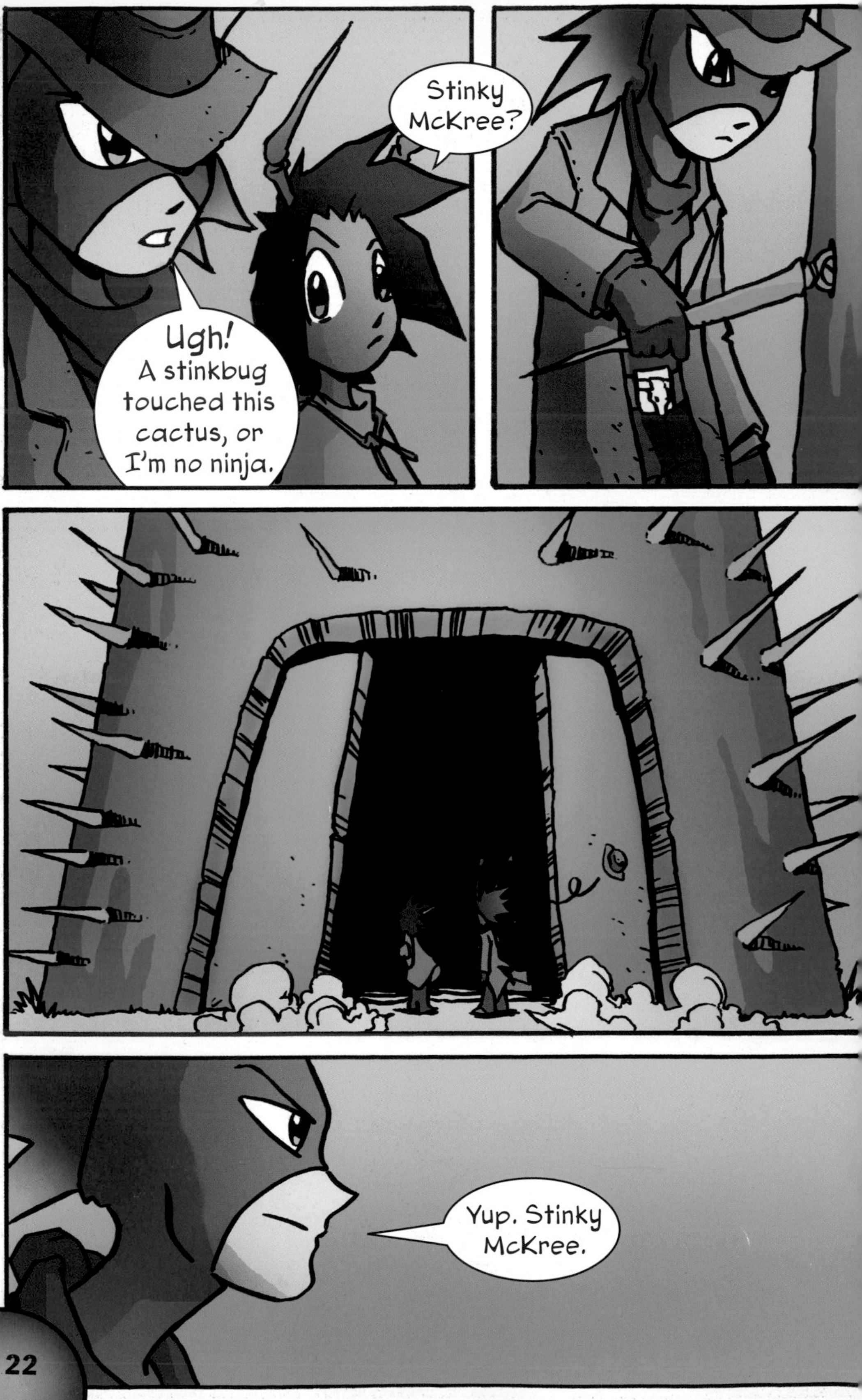
Ugh!
A stinkbug touched this cactus, or I'm no ninja.
Stinky McKree?
Yup. Stinky McKree.

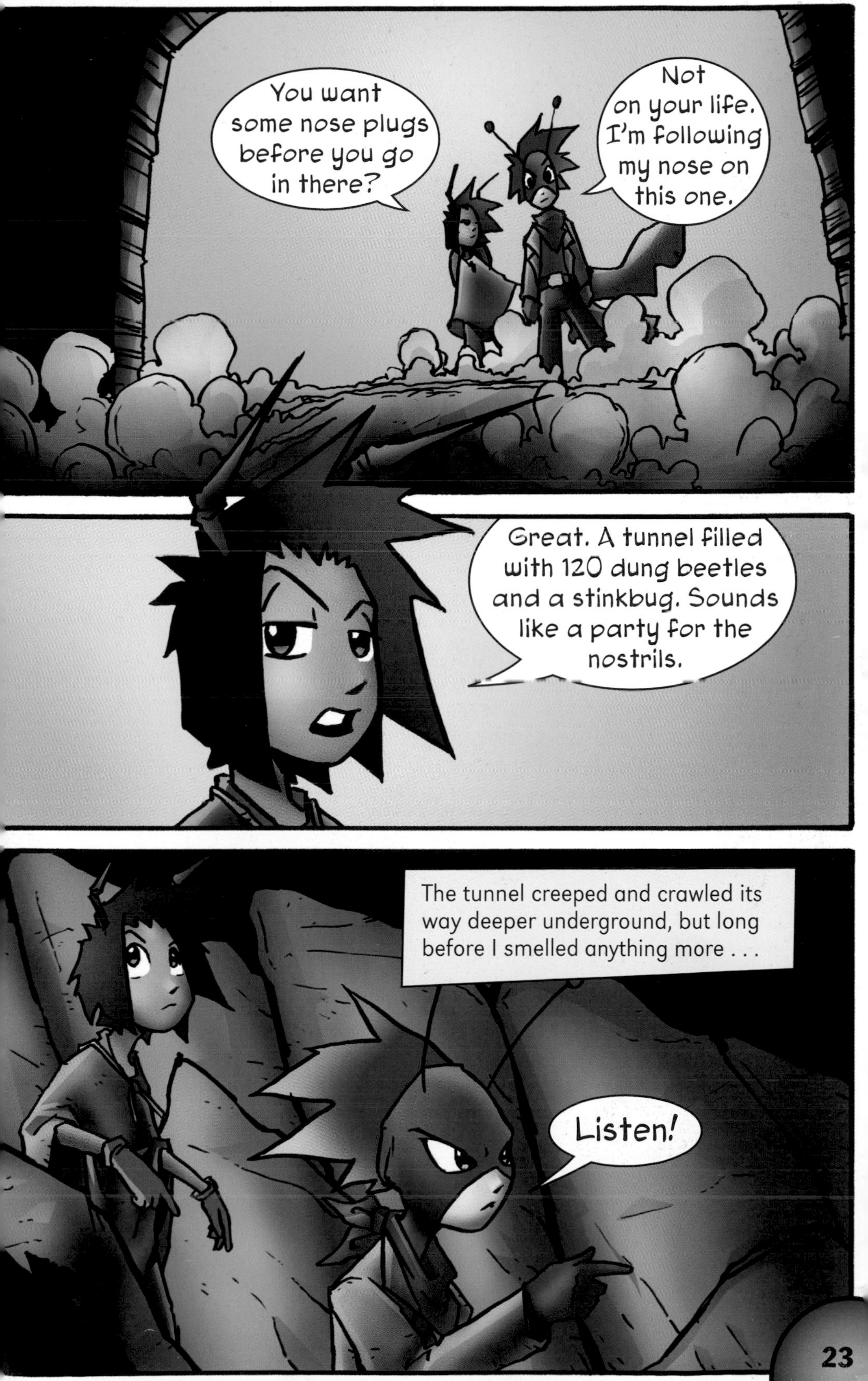
You want some nose plugs before you go in there?
Not on your life. I'm following my nose on this one.
Great. A tunnel filled with 120 dung beetles and a stinkbug. Sounds like a party for the nostrils.
The tunnel creeped and crawled its way deeper underground, but long before I smelled anything more . . .
Listen!

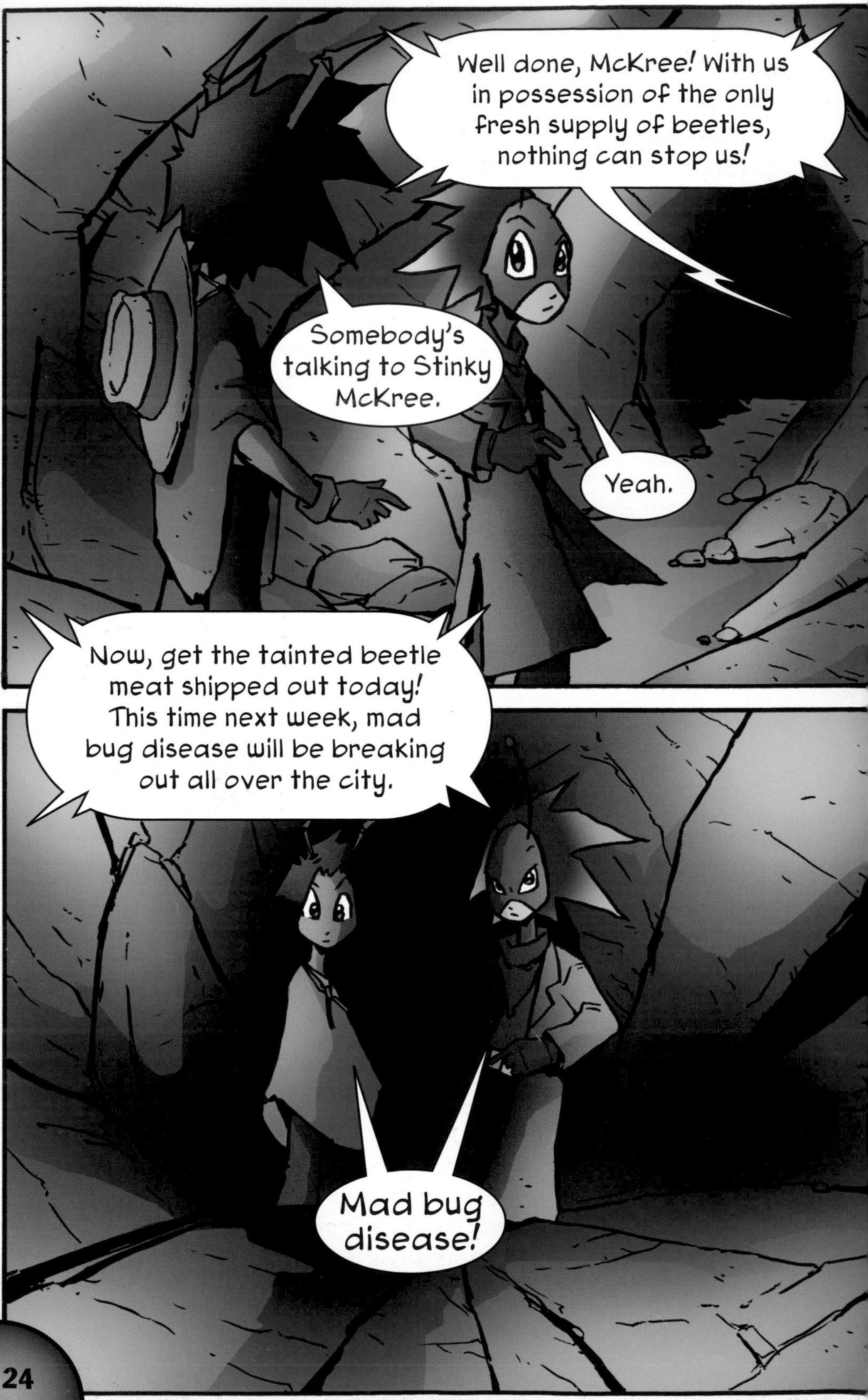
Well done, McKree! With us in possession of the only fresh supply of beetles, nothing can stop us!
Somebody's talking to Stinky McKree.
Yeah.
Now, get the tainted beetle meat shipped out today! This time next week, mad bug disease will be breaking out all over the city.
Mad bug disease!

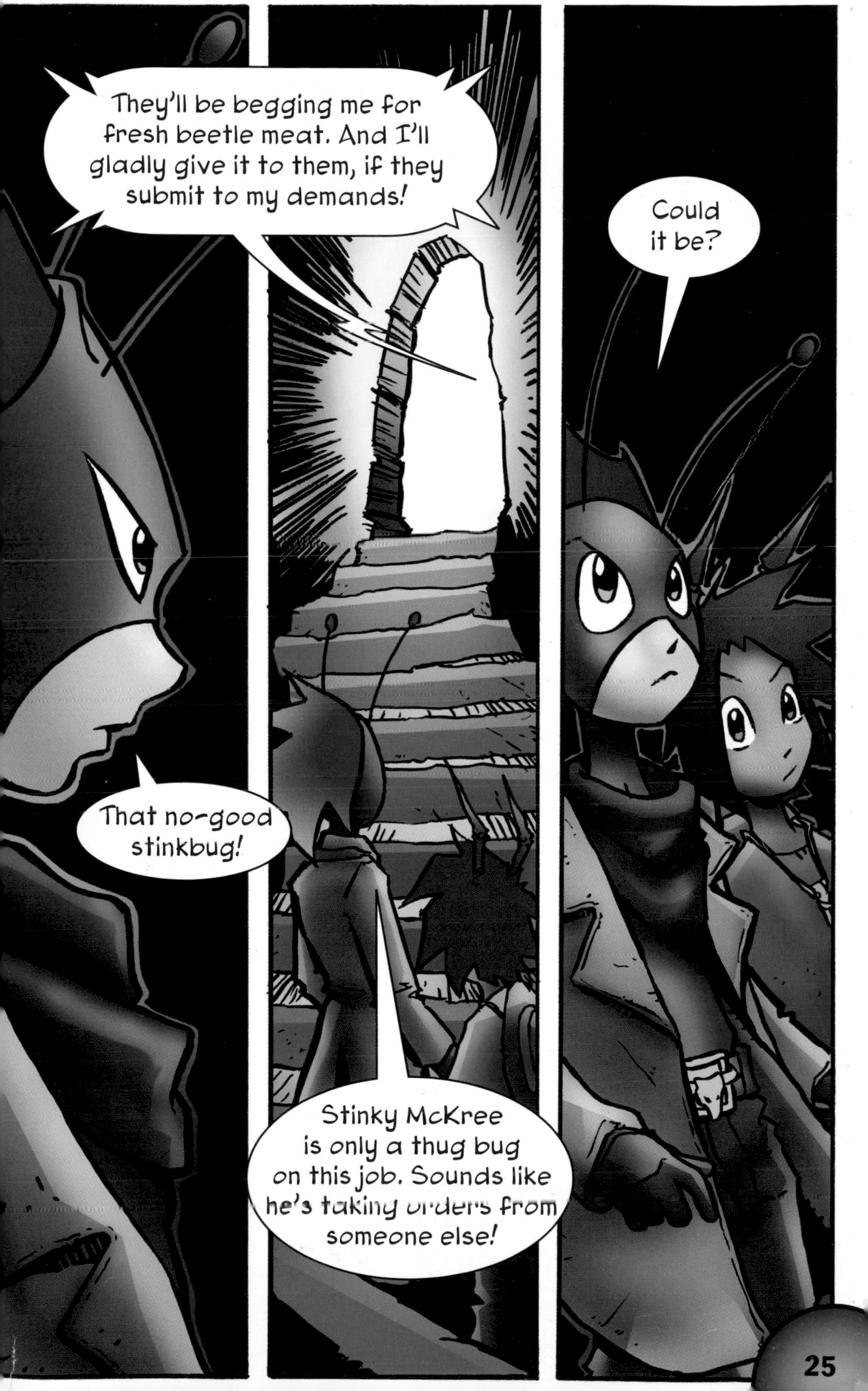
They'll be begging me for fresh beetle meat. And I'll gladly give it to them, if they submit to my demands!
That no-good stinkbug!
Stinky McKree is only a thug bug on this job. Sounds like he's taking orders from someone else!
Could it be?

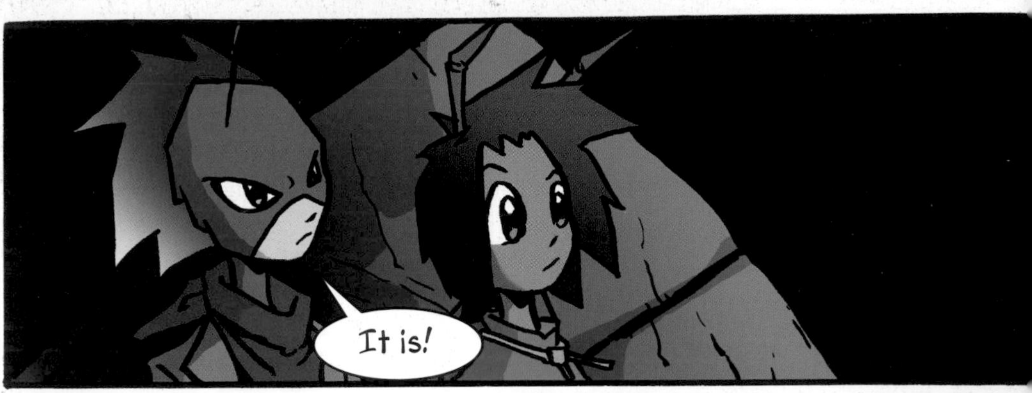
It is!

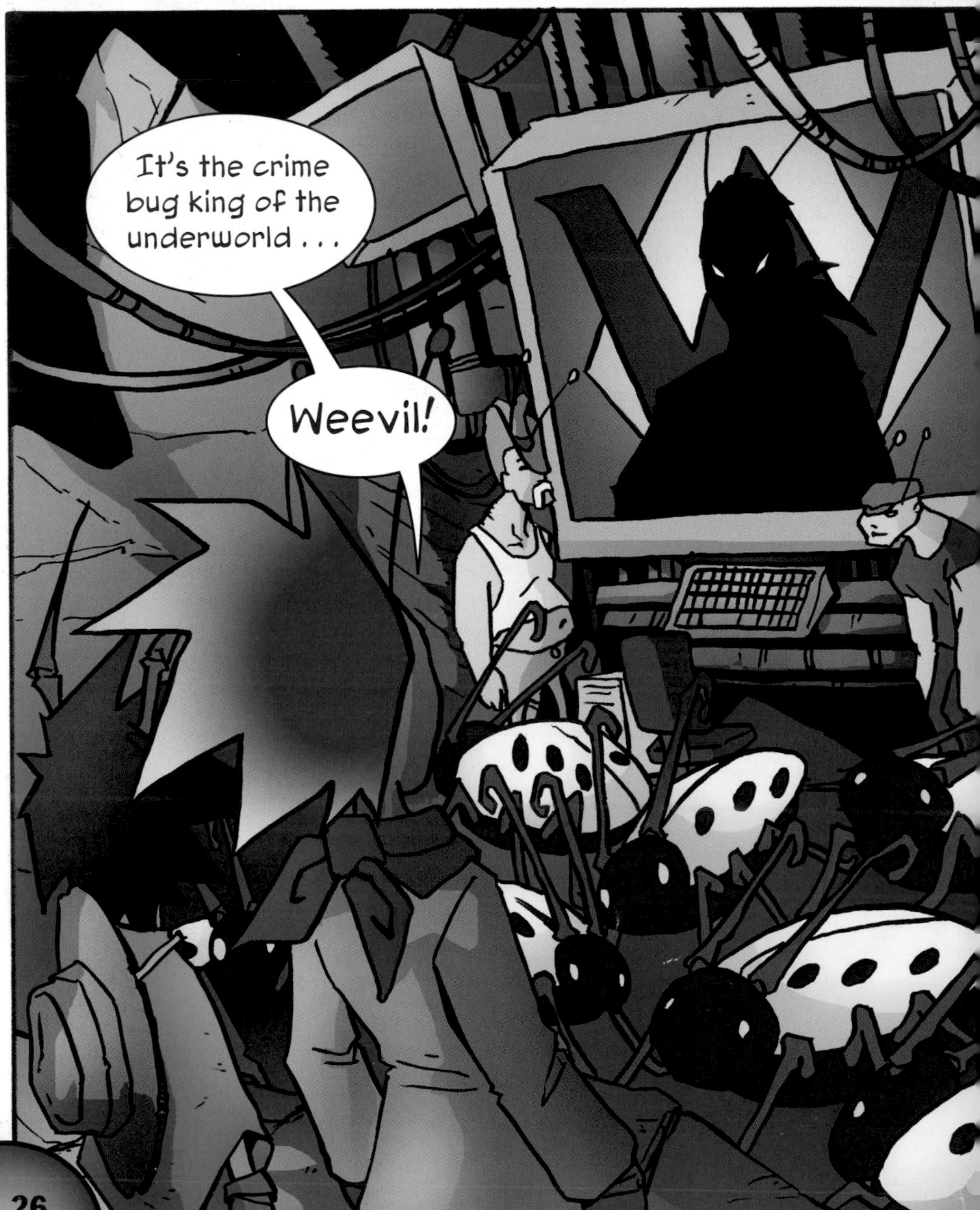
It's the crime bug king of the underworld . . .
Weevil!

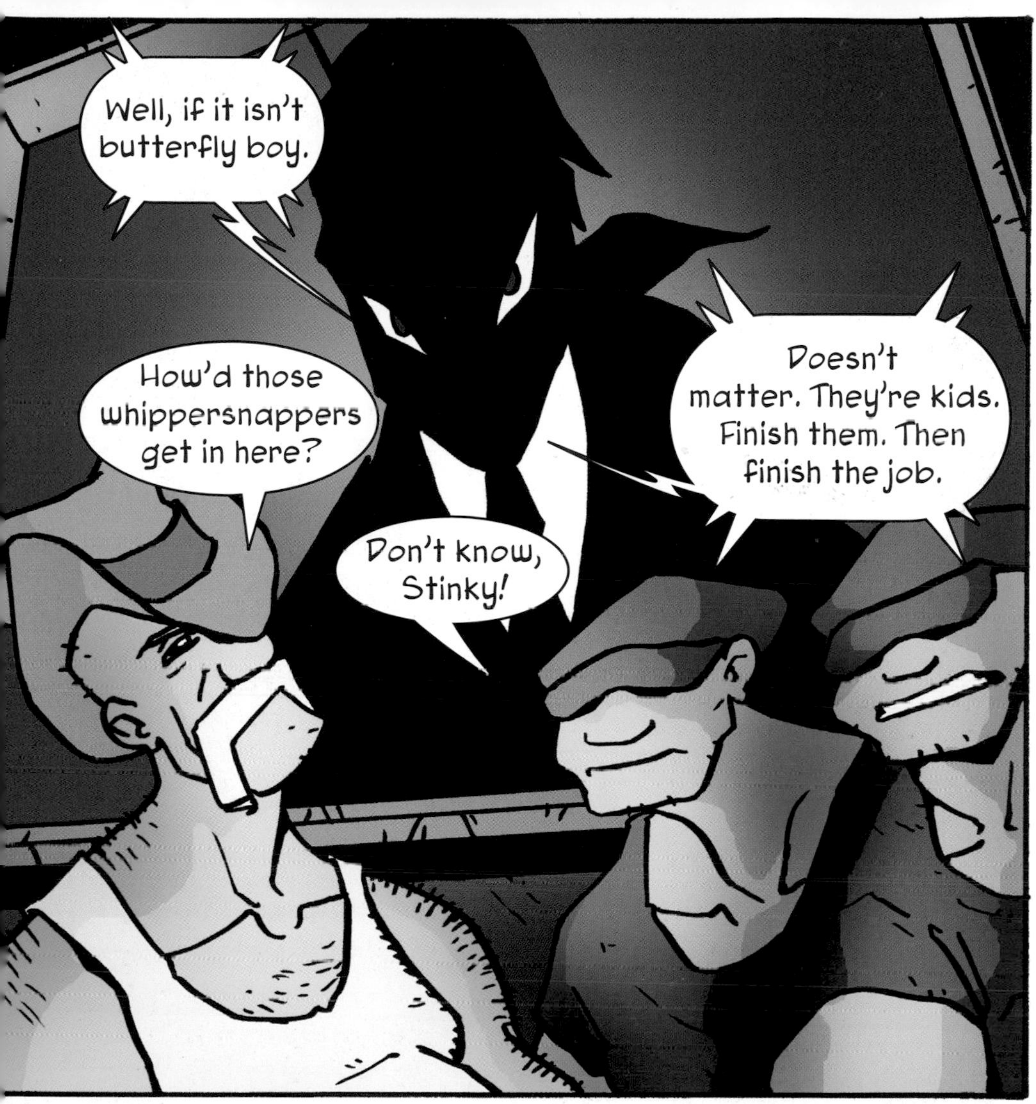
Well, if it isn't butterfly boy.
How'd those whippersnappers get in here?
Doesn't matter. They're kids. Finish them. Then finish the job.
Don't know, Stinky!

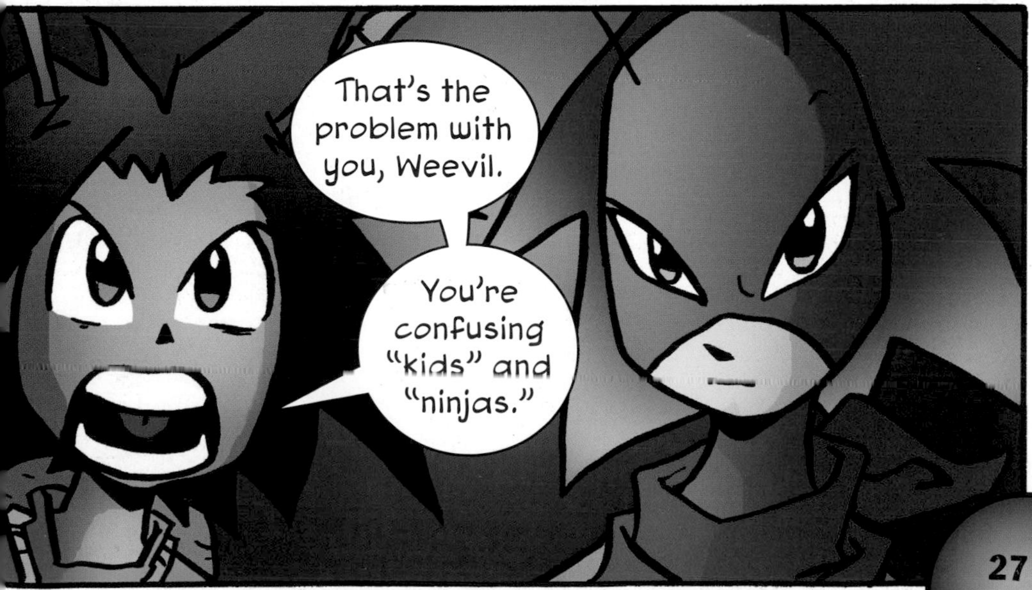
That's the problem with you, Weevil.
You're confusing "kids" and "ninjas."

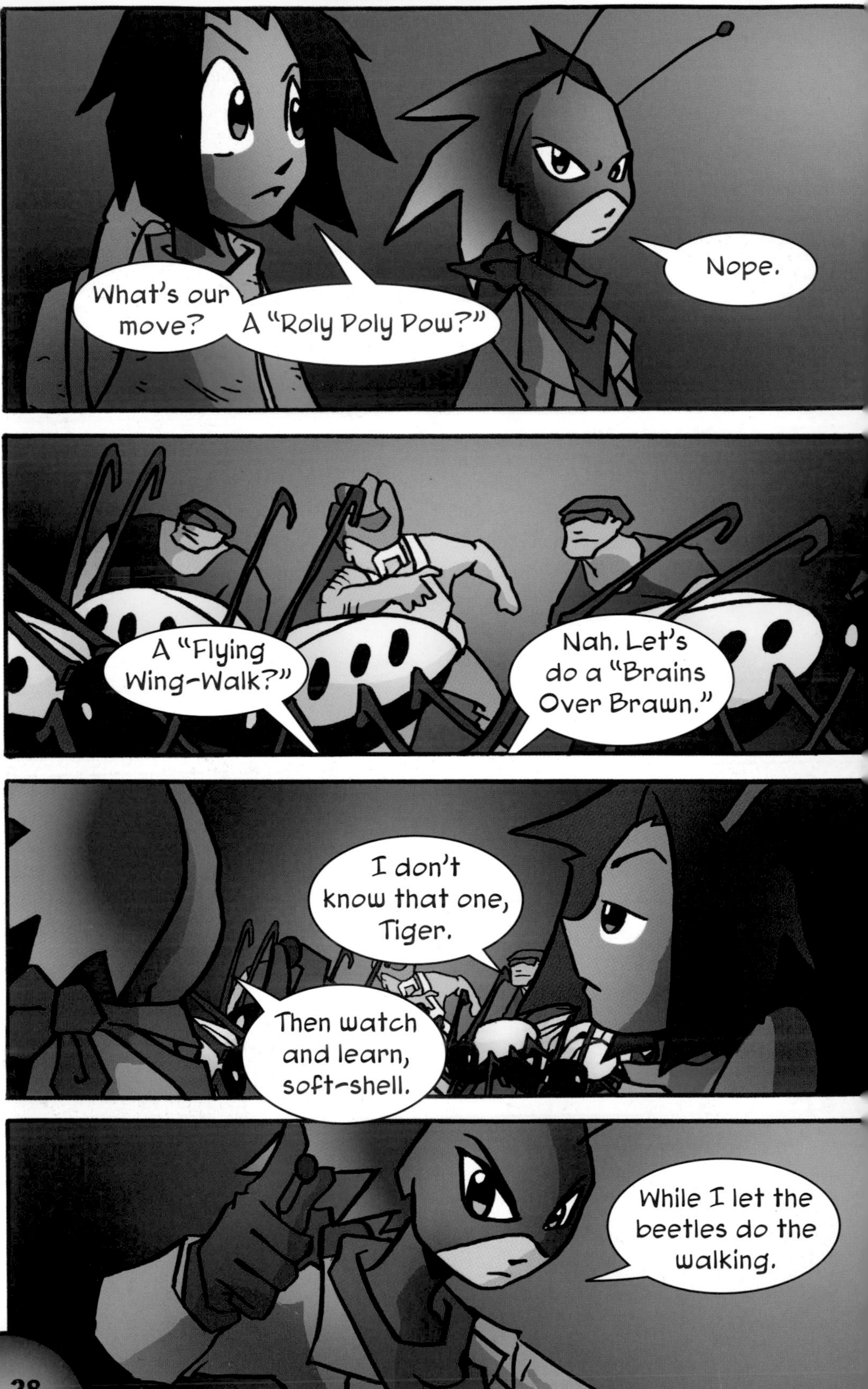
What's our move?
A "Roly Poly Pow?"
Nope.
A "Flying Wing-Walk?"
Nah. Let's do a "Brains Over Brawn."
I don't know that one, Tiger.
Then watch and learn, soft-shell.
While I let the beetles do the walking.

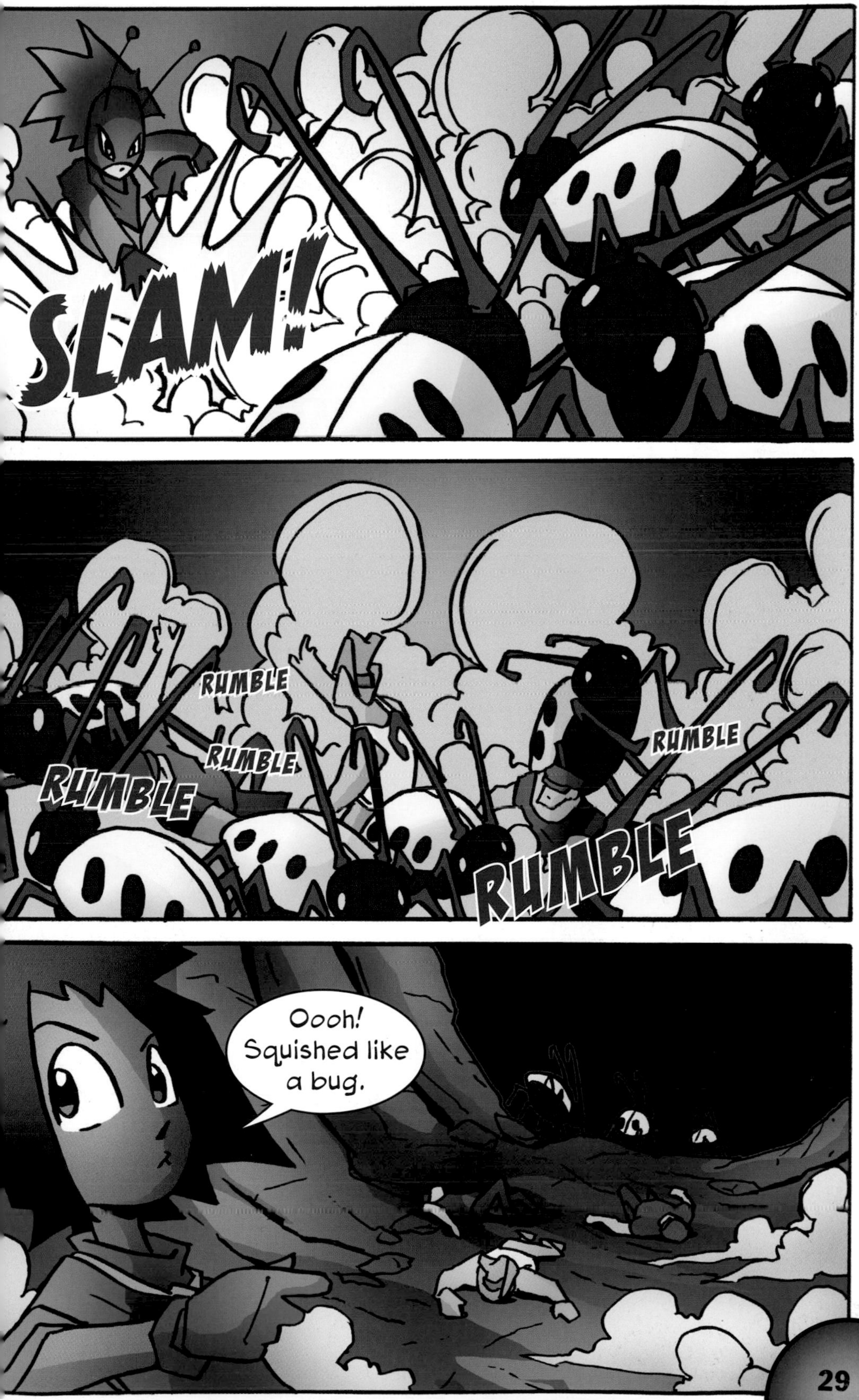
SLAM!
RUMBLE
RUMBLE
RUMBLE
RUMBLE
RUMBLE
Oooh! Squished like a bug.

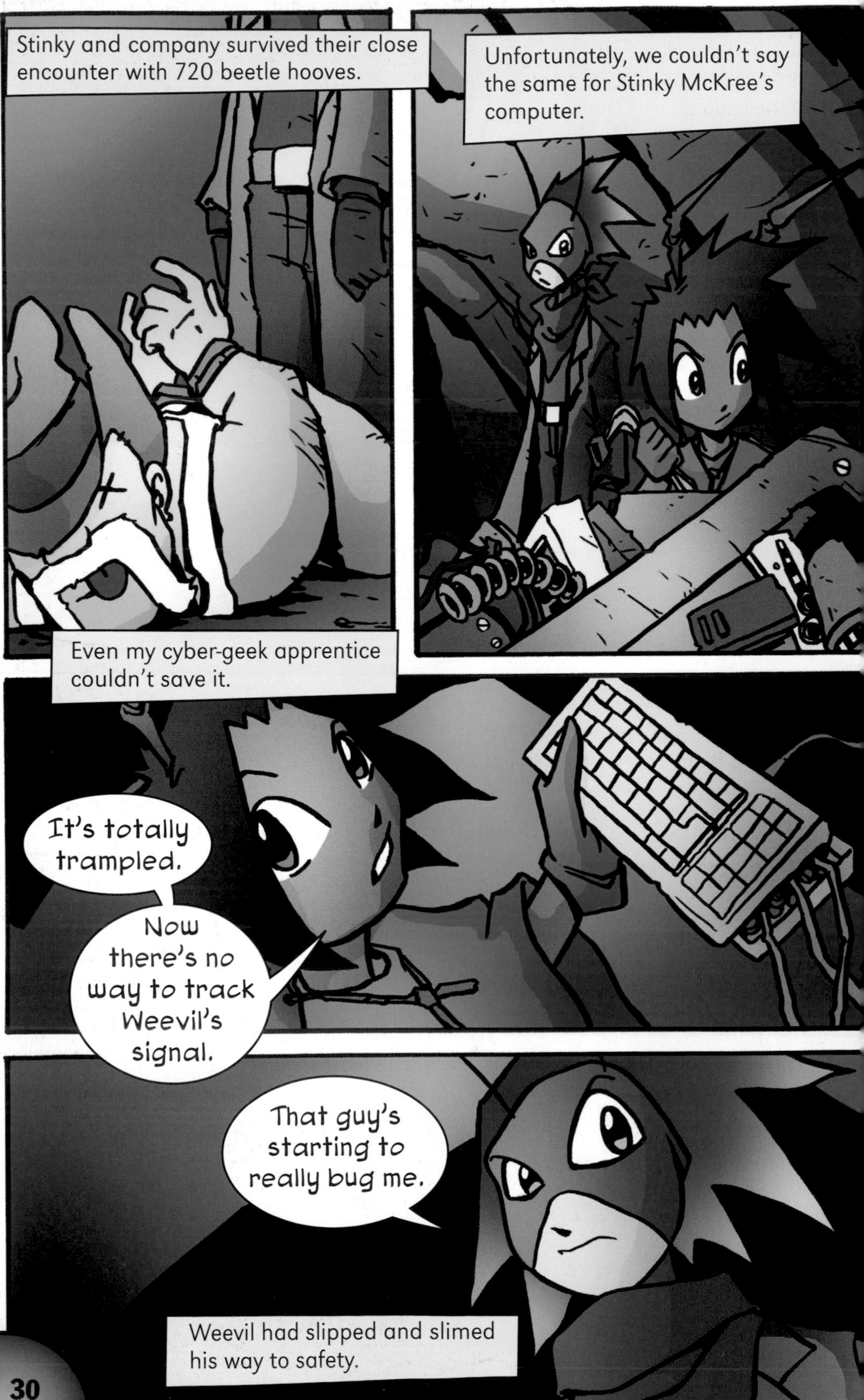
Stinky and company survived their close encounter with 720 beetle hooves.
Unfortunately, we couldn't say the same for Stinky McKree's computer.
Even my cyber-geek apprentice couldn't save it.
It's totally trampled.
Now there's no way to track Weevil's signal.
That guy's starting to really bug me.
Weevil had slipped and slimed his way to safety.

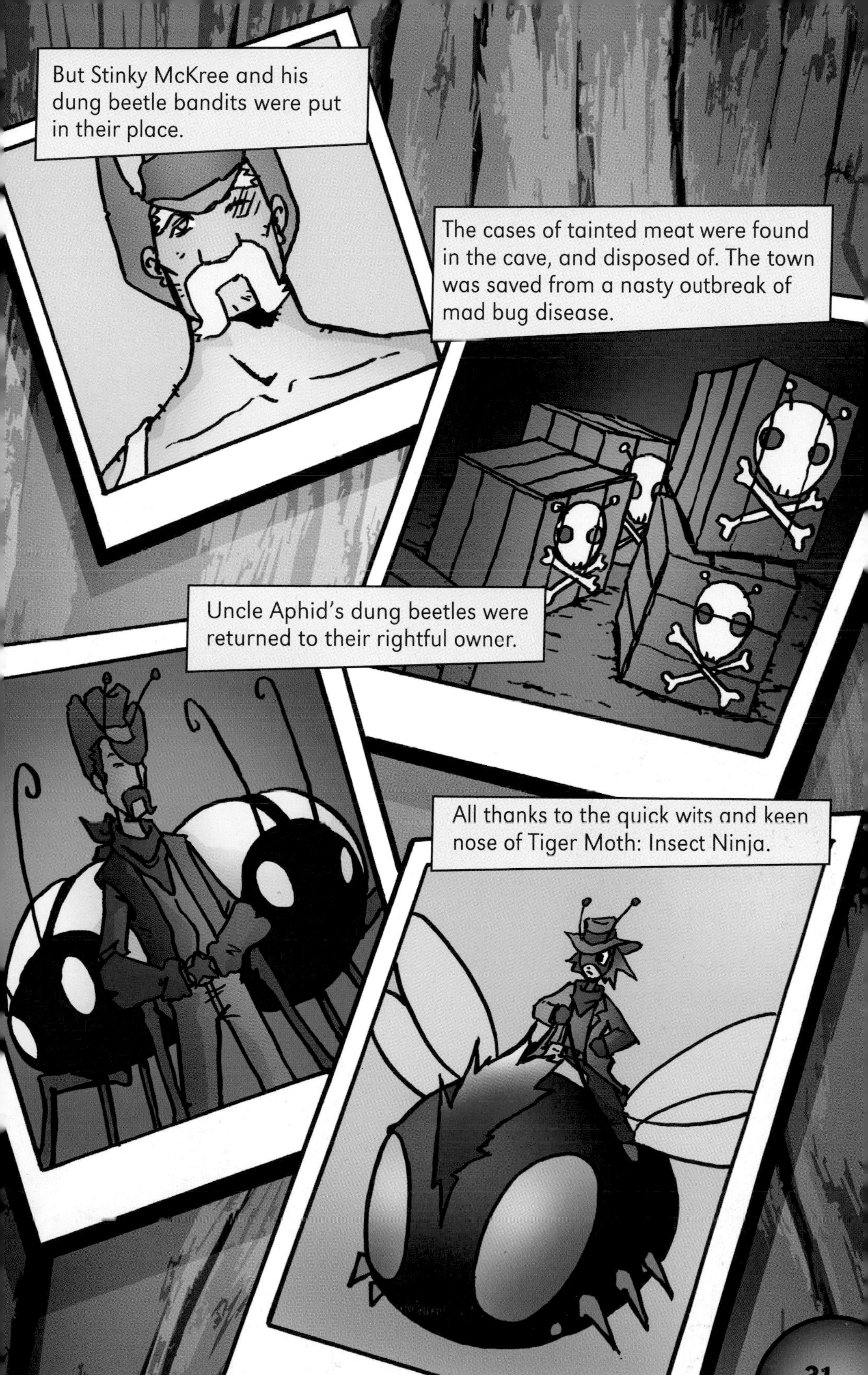
But Stinky McKree and his dung beetle bandits were put in their place.
The cases of tainted meat were found in the cave, and disposed of. The town was saved from a nasty outbreak of mad bug disease.
Uncle Aphid's dung beetles were returned to their rightful owner.
All thanks to the quick wits and keen nose of Tiger Moth: Insect Ninja.

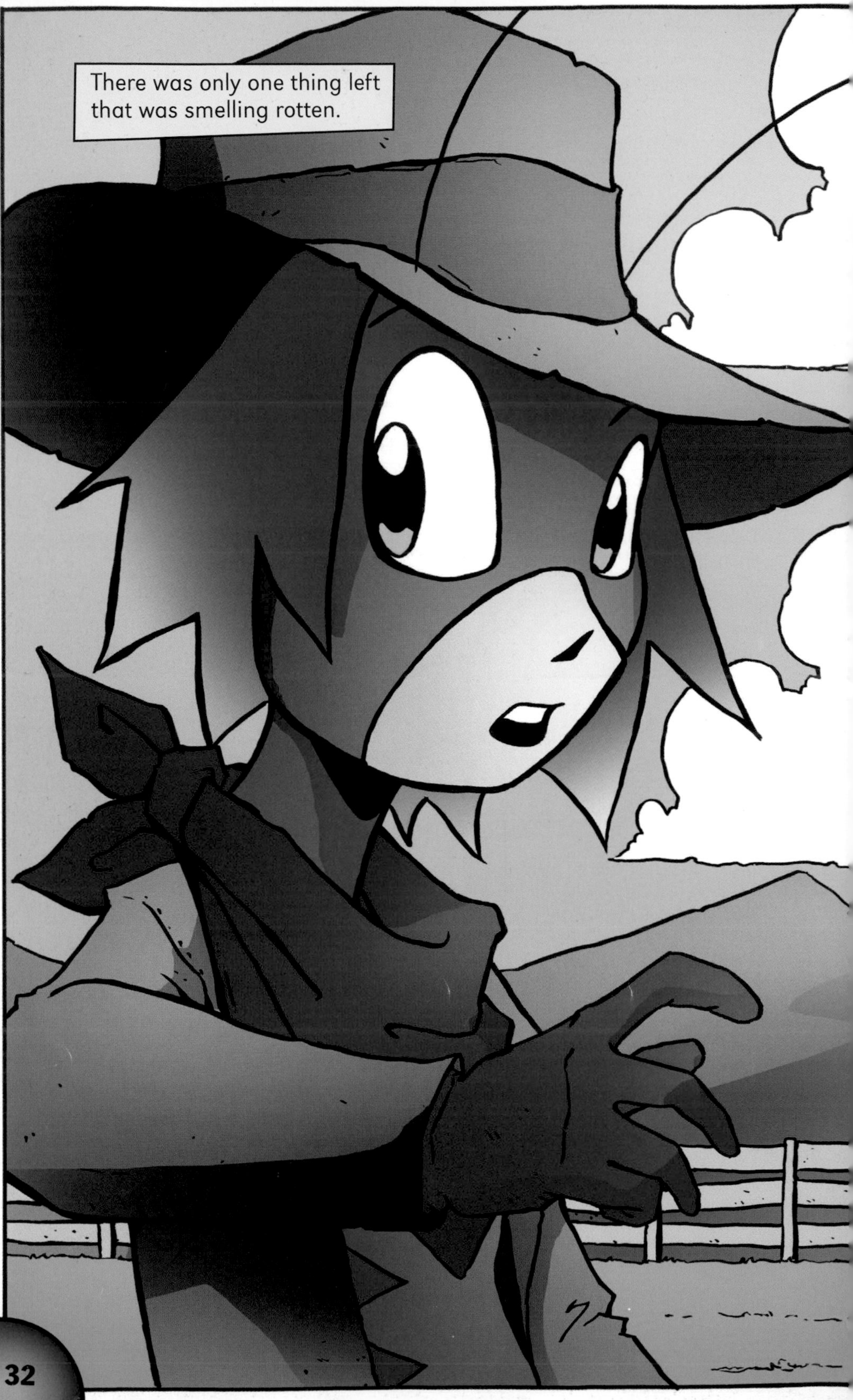
There was only one thing left that was smelling rotten.

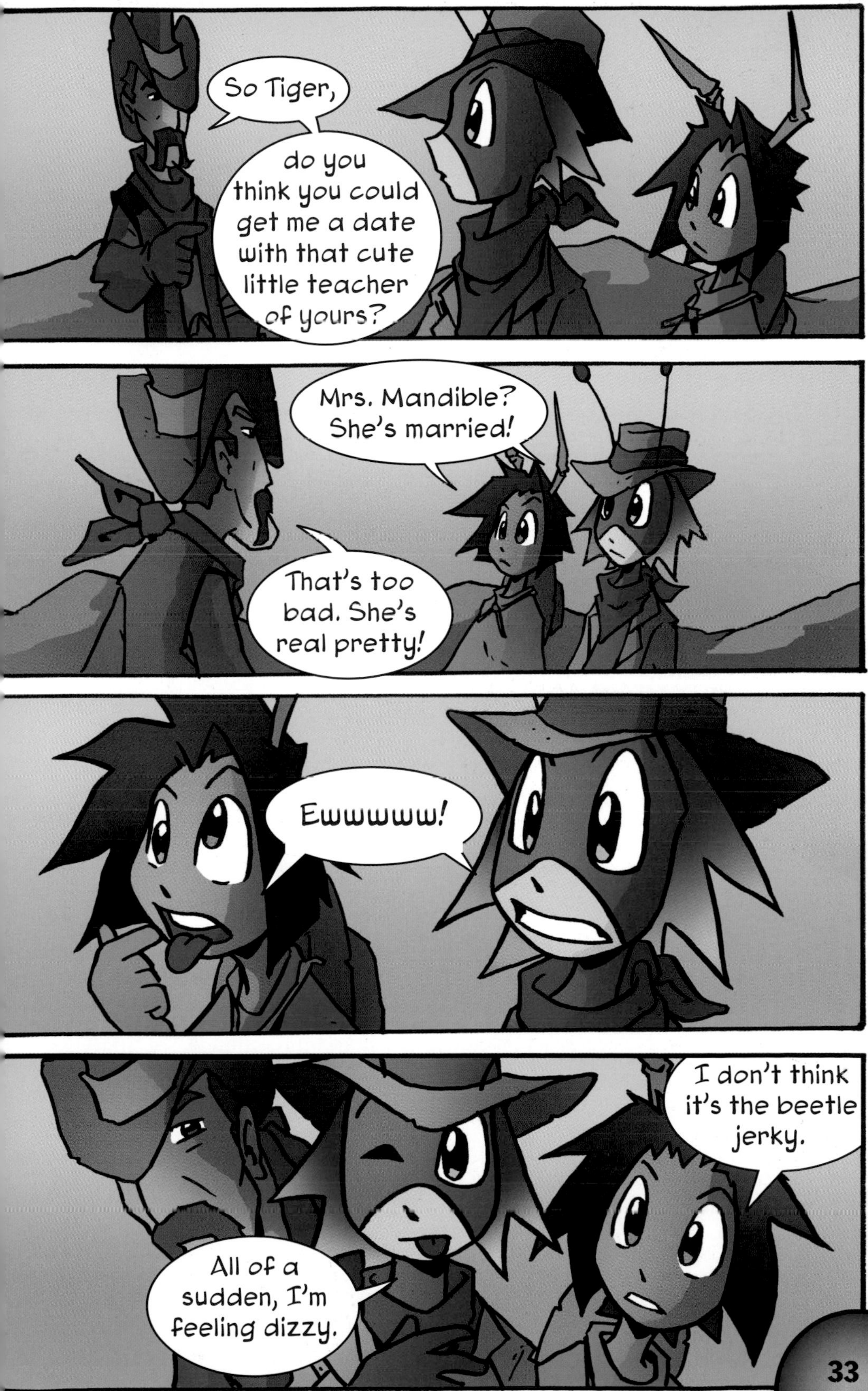
So Tiger,
do you think you could get me a date with that cute little teacher of yours?
Mrs. Mandible? She's married!
That's too bad. She's real pretty!
Ewwwww!
I don't think it's the beetle jerky.
All of a sudden, I'm feeling dizzy.

ABOUT THE AUTHOR

Aaron Reynolds loves bugs and loves books, so Tiger Moth was a perfect blend of both. Aaron is the author of several great books for kids, including *Chicks and Salsa*, which *Publishers Weekly* called "a literary fandango" that "even confirmed macaroni-and-cheese lovers will devour." Aaron had no idea what a "fandango" was, but after looking it up in the dictionary (it means "playful and silly behavior"), he hopes to write several more fandangos in the future. He lives near Chicago with his wife, two kids, and four insect-obsessed cats.

ABOUT THE ILLUSTRATOR

Erik Lervold was born in Puerto Rico, a small island in the Caribbean, and has been a professional painter. He attended college at the University of Puerto Rico's Mayaguez campus, where he majored in Civil Engineering. Deciding that he wanted to be a full-time artist, he moved to Florida, New York, Chicago, Duluth, and finally Minneapolis. He attended the Minneapolis College of Art and Design, majored in Comic Art, and graduated in 2004. Erik teaches classes in libraries in the Minneapolis area, and has taught art in the Minnesota Children's Museum. He loves the color green and has a bunch of really big goggles. He also loves sandwiches. If you want him to be your friend, bring him a roast beef sandwich and he will love you forever.

GLOSSARY

aphid (AY-fid)-a bug that that sucks juice out of plants, like a cactus or a yucca plant

bronco (BRONG-ko)-a cowboy name for a horse that lives out on the desert

corral (kor-AL)-a fenced area to keep horses or cattle or dung beetles

cringe (KRINJ)-to shrink away from something in fear. People who don't like beetles or aphids, might cringe when they see them.

rustle (RUS-uhl)-to steal horses or cattle (or dung beetles)

scallywag (SKAL-ee-wag)-cowboy talk for a **varmint**. See below.

taint (TAYNT)-to make something yucky or sick

vamoosed (va-MOOST)-cowboy talk for gone, vanished, or run away

varmint (VAR-mint)-cowboy talk for a criminal or bad person

whippersnapper (WIP-ur-snap-ur)-a grownup word for a kid who's noisy or energetic; a brat or a super hero.

FROM THE NINJA NOTEBOOK

Dung Beetles and Other Desert Bugs

Dung beetles get their name from their habit of feeding on dung, or animal waste products.

Some dung beetles called rollers, use their back legs to roll dung into a smooth, tiny ball.

Ranchers like dung beetles. The little critters move the dung away from the cattle who made it. Since dung can attract flies and other bugs, the dung beetles keep the cattle free from pests.

The ancient Egyptians believed that the sun was rolled across the sky by a gigantic dung beetle named Khepri.

The deadliest bug in the U.S. desert is the Black Widow spider. A female Black Widow is 15 times more poisonous than a rattlesnake!

Desert tarantulas are hairy spiders that grow up to 3 inches long and live in the Southwestern United States. They are non-poisonous and make great house pets!

Yucca moths are very helpful to the yucca plants. Without the tiny fliers, the prickly yuccas would not get pollinated.

Darkling beetles have a cool way of getting water in the dry desert. Drops of early morning fog turn into liquid on their smooth, shiny front wings.

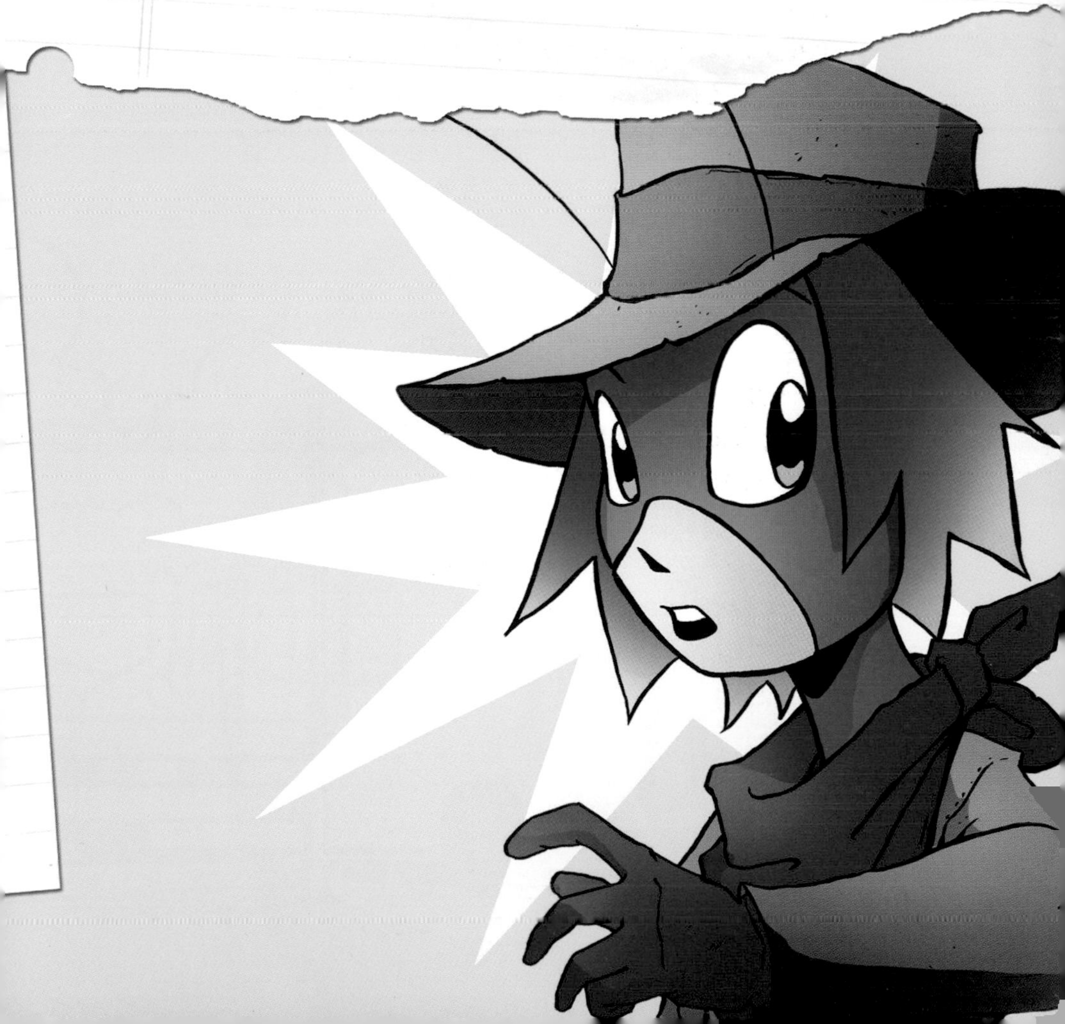

DISCUSSION QUESTIONS

1. Have you ever been on a field trip to a farm or a ranch? Would you like to go on one? Why or why not?

2. Uncle Aphid seems like a cool uncle. Do you have any relatives that have unusual jobs or live in unusual places?

3. Tiger Moth and Kung Pow are both eager to help Uncle Aphid find his dung beetles. But Kung Pow isn't very excited about being out in the country. Why don't you think he likes cowboy life as much as Tiger Moth seems to?

WRITING PROMPTS

1. Imagine you can ride a horsefly just like Tiger Moth and Kung Pow. Where would you fly? What does it feel like? Is the buzzing of the wings too loud for you to hear other sounds? Write a description of your amazing flight.

2. Kung Pow does not like getting stinkbug goo on his hand. He wants to wash it off right away. Have you ever gotten real dirty working on a chore? Write what the chore was and how you had to clean up.

3. Uncle Aphid is very upset when he finds his dung beetles have been rustled. Have you ever lost something that meant a lot to you? Do you know someone who had something stolen? Write and tell what happened.

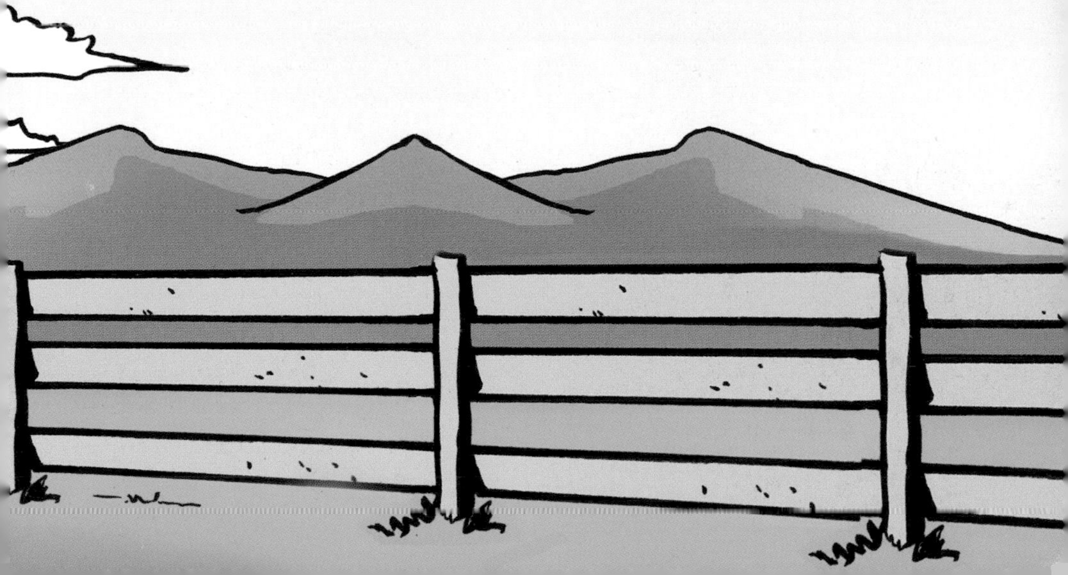

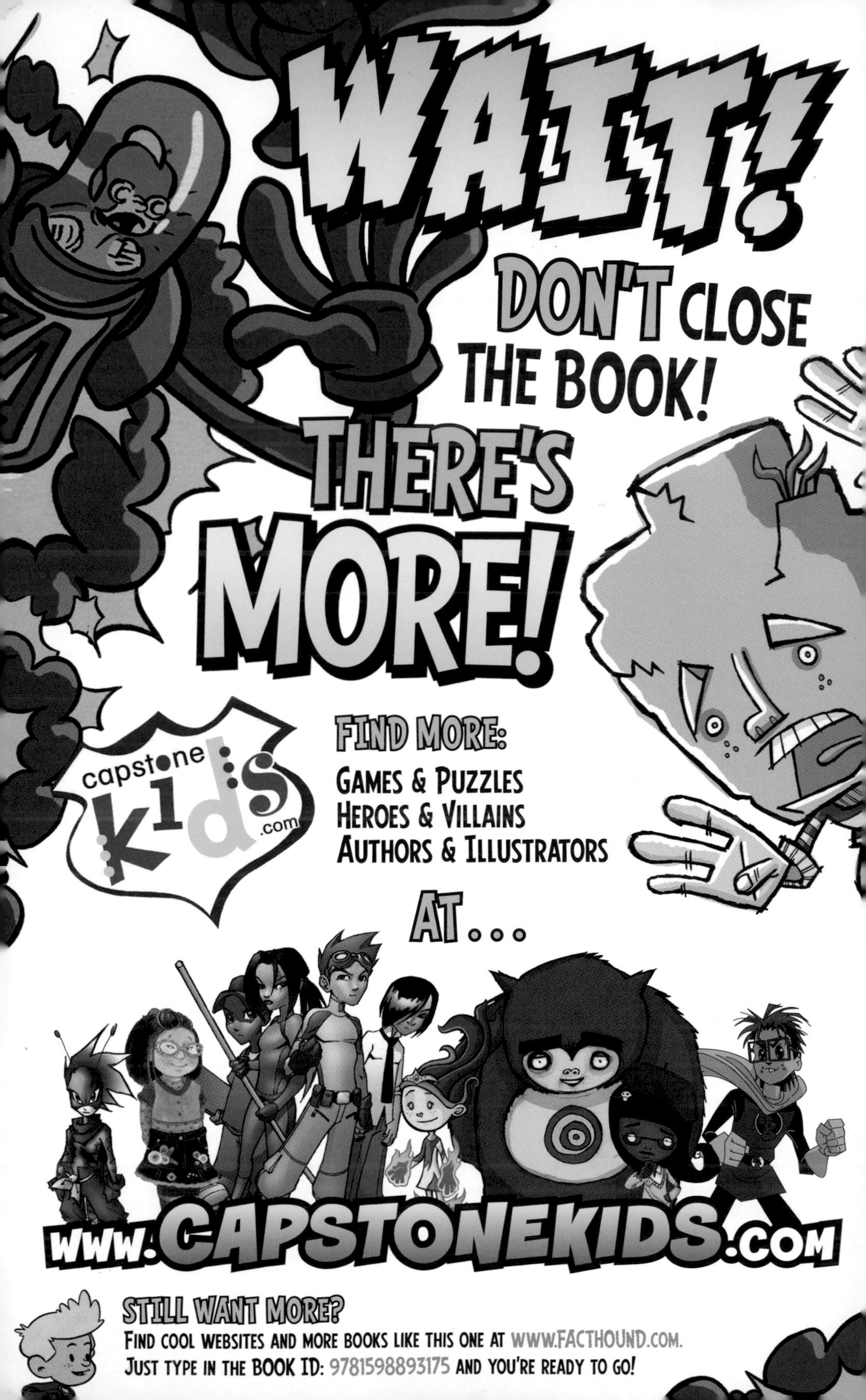
WAIT!
DON'T CLOSE THE BOOK!
THERE'S MORE!
capstone kids .com
FIND MORE:
GAMES & PUZZLES
HEROES & VILLAINS
AUTHORS & ILLUSTRATORS
AT...
WWW.CAPSTONEKIDS.COM
STILL WANT MORE?
FIND COOL WEBSITES AND MORE BOOKS LIKE THIS ONE AT WWW.FACTHOUND.COM.
JUST TYPE IN THE BOOK ID: 9781598893175 AND YOU'RE READY TO GO!